Dedication

In Memory of Aunt Ruth

I0741691

Portrait of a Ghost

Betty Ann Harris

Print ISBNs

Amazon print 9780228636564
Ingram Spark 9780228636595
Barnes & Noble9780228636571
BWL Print 9780228636588

(BWL Publishing logo- a gold globe-Books we love to write...Authors around the world)

Copyright 2025 by Betty Ann Harris
Editor Nancy M. Bell
Cover artist Michelle Lee

Table of Contents

Prologue

Mystic Port, an old and historic New England seaport town, was settled in the late 1700's by a group of strong-willed and courageous French colonists who fled their beloved France during the horrors of the years-long French Revolution. America had already won their independence, and settlements were popping up all over the coast of New England. These French settlers yearned for the freedoms the colonists from America had so gallantly fought for and ultimately won. Many, just wanted to escape their war-ravaged country and start their lives anew in a place where they could flourish, raise their families, and worship as they pleased. The French Revolution was marked by extreme repression, executions, and massacres ordered by the government that resulted in a significant and catastrophic loss of life. Many were lucky to have escaped from France with their lives.

During the upheaval and revolution in France, a young French woman by the name of Monique Garnier was hoping to be able to flee from France. She had lost both her brothers in a skirmish with some revolutionary government soldiers and now feared for her own life. A friend of her deceased brothers told her to get out of France while she still could, as things were only going to get worse. She was hoping to be able to get passage to America on the ship Liberté.

The grueling journey had taken her nearly a month after fleeing Vendres to finally reach Port Collioure, and thankfully, just in time as the ship was due to deport the following day. Part of her journey had been on foot, and part in a carriage owned by a wealthy aristocrat, who was by no means a gentleman. He suffered a massive coronary and died while trying to seduce Monique, a woman young enough to be his daughter. Claude Benoit's driver, Pierre DuPont, buried his boss by the side of the road, and by the grace of God, took pity on poor Monique. He drove her the rest of the way to Collioure and gave her Benoit's purse so she'd have enough money to pay for her passage to America.

Thankfully, when she reached the shipyard in Collioure, there were many other French citizens there, families and some others traveling alone. A young Frenchmen asked if he could be of assistance to Monique. As it turned out, he was also waiting in line to pay for passage on the ship Liberte to Boston. After Monique paid the fare, the couple parted company, as they would be in different quarters on the ship. She thanked him for his kindness.

As harrowing as her trip to Collioure had been, the voyage was even more dreadful, as the weather was awful and the sea churned angrily much of the time. The conditions on board the ship were best described as ghastly. Poor Monique could not imagine living in the abhorrent conditions for even a day, let alone the months it would take to cross the Atlantic and arrive in Boston in America. She ended up spending most of her time below deck retching. She was seriously wondering if this decision to sail to America had been a terrible mistake.

The nights were the worst. It was almost impossible to sleep and Monique was only able to do so when she was so tired that she passed out due to sheer exhaustion. There were also others who were ill, and the stench beneath deck was becoming intolerable. Monique became quite depressed. She was beginning to wonder whether she'd survive long enough to make it America.

Thankfully, the kind, young man she met before the ship set sail, named Jean-Claude Beaudicort, befriended Monique and quite possibly saved her life. Monique, unable to take much food during the first part of the voyage, was weak and becoming despondent. Jean-Claude would visit her almost everyday and he looked after her, making sure she had enough water to drink. He would engage her in conversation to keep her mind off the terrible conditions in the quarters she shared with other passengers. After several weeks of Jean-Claude caring for her, Monique was finally able to take some food, and became strong enough to be escorted on short walks on the deck with him in the mornings. The sea finally calmed and two and a half long months later, the ship Liberté finally docked in Boston Harbor.

During the long voyage, Monique had fallen in love with Jean-Claude, and he with her. They decided they would be married as soon as they were settled in America. Monique and Jean-Claude were married on June 25th, 1794. They settled in Mystic Port, Rhode Island. With the help of Jean-Claude's cousin, Pierre, they built a small home on property adjoining Pierre's farmstead. They grew mostly vegetables like corn, beans and squash, for their own use to feed their families. They also raised chickens and ducks.

Life was hard, but they thrived despite periods of drought and other hardships that came with living in a mostly undeveloped land. In 1795, Monique gave birth to her first child, a son they named Henry. Four more babies would be born in the coming years, two more boys and two girls.

Chapter One

Prudence Trivit walked the all too familiar path from her historic and stately Victorian Queen Anne home to the majestic Mystic Port Museum and Library where she worked. She imagined herself as the beautiful heroine, Catherine, from the latest historical romance novel she was reading. Catherine, besides being a stunning beauty, was intelligent, witty, and not at all shy. Prudence, known as Prudy by her family and the few close friends she had, was considered to be extremely intelligent. But that's the only similarity Prudy felt there was between Catherine and herself.

Prudy knew there were many townspeople, especially those who didn't really know her, who thought she was a just a geek and described her as that uptight woman who worked at the museum and library. On more than one occasion she'd witnessed a small group of townspeople, mostly some high school aged girls, laughing and whispering about her when she walked by. They would call her Prudy the Prude. She would sometimes hear their whispers and snide remarks. Being on the sensitive side, of course this bothered Prudy. If only they would take the time to get to know her and just give her half a chance, she was fairly certain they'd like her. But Prudy also realistically knew that many of the townspeople would never give her that chance. Mostly because of who was in her family tree, and rumored, inaccurate history. Prudy was just reserved and shy. She'd been pretty much of a loner most of her life.

In reality, Prudy was not a prude at all. Actually, quite the opposite was true as she was an intelligent, warm, and compassionate woman. But she longed to actually live a life that was full of exciting experiences. Maybe the types of experiences the heroines often had in the historical romance novels she read. She dreamed of romance and adventure, trips to exotic places, having high tea in London or champagne in Paris. And of course, being accompanied on these adventures by a handsome and witty young man.

Prudy was the town librarian and historian, known for constantly having her head in a book. With reading glasses perched on her nose and her hair pulled tightly back, she looked every part the prim and proper librarian. Her dark gray, very plain linen suit further accentuated her strait-laced appearance.

Her Aunt Magnolia, called Maggie by almost everyone in Mystic Port, often suggested that Prudy let her hair down, wear her contact lenses, and dress a bit less conservatively. Maybe then she would appear more approachable. And possibly, once people got to know her, they would see the beauty within and the kind and compassionate heart she possessed.

Deep in thought and not paying much attention, Prudy stepped on a stone lying on the sidewalk. Her foot rolled over and she almost lost her balance and fell. She desperately fought to keep herself upright. Two high school aged girls on the other side of the street snickered and then giggled out loud at her unfortunate mishap. Steadying herself, Prudy ignored them and continued on her way. She didn't have time to deal with such petty and immature nonsense. Especially not today.

This particular morning, she arrived early to work. Prudy wanted to prepare for her meeting with a reporter from The Coastal Press, who would be eager to glean her knowledge of the history of the town of Mystic Port. This summer marked the town's 250th anniversary, and a huge parade, celebrations and a magnificent gala and ball at the museum would be taking place over the Labor Day weekend. The town was abuzz with excitement and anticipation.

Prudy fumbled through the numerous keys on her large, brass key ring until she found the right one to unlock the massive front door to the old, Italianate mansion, which served as the library and historical society headquarters, as well as housing the museum for the quaint, old seaport town of Mystic Port. The historic mansion was huge and quite impressive, with a ballroom that had original gasoliers and chandeliers, and an entire wall of original French doors that led out to an expansive portico and beautiful gardens beyond. It was a massive and majestic building, and the pride of the citizens of Mystic Port. Prudy loved her job and took it seriously. She really couldn't imagine doing anything else. But as much as she loved her job, she did feel that something was missing.

Now that she had the right key, Prudy thought about her somewhat lonely life, wondering if she'd ever find someone who shared her interests, especially her passion for American and European history. Or perhaps a well-educated, but attractive, man who enjoyed literature and reading as much as she did. She yearned to have an in-depth conversation with someone about something other than the weather or sports, or the latest gossip from the entertainment industry.

Ironically, Prudy rather enjoyed sports or a good movie, but she wanted much more than that; maybe some romance and adventure. Prudy decided right at that moment that she was going to take her aunt's advice, expand her horizons and improve her appearance and sense of style, or the lack thereof. And to get started, she'd check out the beauty and fashion magazines in the library during her lunch hour.

As she organized things at her desk, Prudy glanced at her watch and realized she still had thirty minutes before she needed to open the library and before Mr. Monroe was due to arrive. The sudden ringing of the library phone startled her. It was quite unusual for someone to be calling the library, especially before it was due to open. She hoped it was not an emergency or bad news. Anxiously she answered, "Good morning, Mystic Port Library, Miss Trivit speaking."

"Good morning, Miss Trivit. This is Dylan Monroe from the Coastal Press. How are you this beautiful morning?"

"Oh...yes, Mr. Monroe, I'm fine, thank you. May I help you? You're not lost, are you?"

"No, I'm actually here in Mystic Port already and I was just stopping by the Brew Awhile Coffee House to pick up my morning cup of Joe and wondered if you might like me to pick up a cup for you as well. That is if you drink coffee. Or I could get you tea if you prefer."

Taken a bit off guard, Prudy answered hesitantly in the affirmative. "Yes...please, a small black coffee would be great, and thank you, Mr. Monroe."

"Please, call me Dylan. And may I call you Prudence?"

"Oh well...um...my friends call me Prudy."

"Very well, Prudy. Then I'll see you soon. I'm looking forward to meeting you and for our interview."

Prudy slowly lowered the phone, placing it gently down on its receiver. She wondered about this Dylan Monroe, as she was not used to someone being so courteous to her, especially a person of the male persuasion, and a perfect stranger. Prudy imagined what Mr. Monroe would think of her once he met her in person. Too bad she hadn't thought of the makeover idea just a bit sooner. Glancing at her watch, she realized she had a few minutes so she could go to the ladies' room and put on some lip gloss and maybe a bit of blush and a touch of mascara. As she opened the door to the ladies' room, she found herself now actually anticipating her meeting with Dylan Monroe. A twinge of excitement settled in the pit of her stomach. He sounded so nice on the phone.

Standing in front of the single mirror that hung on the drab gray wall, she rooted around the bottom of her purse until she found the one tube of tinted lip gloss she carried with her and applied it to her lips. Then she found her makeup case and put on some blush and a touch of mascara. As she glanced in the mirror, she was still dismayed with her prim and proper librarian appearance. She pulled the collar of her plain white, silk blouse to sit over the neckline of her suit jacket, as she had seen done in a French fashion magazine. Peering at herself again, she was still not satisfied. Those glasses had to go. She really only needed them sometimes for reading but had gotten in the habit of just leaving them on all the time. They were usually perched towards the tip of her nose so she could look over them when she didn't need them to read something. She removed them and put them in her pocket, just in case she'd need them to read something during the meeting with Dylan Monroe. As she turned to leave the ladies room, she took one final glance in the mirror and grimaced as she looked at her hair pulled so tightly back. It made her look harsh and older than her actual years. In one decisive movement, she untethered her hair and let it down, allowing it to cascade over her shoulders. Doing so gave her an incredible sense of freedom. She combed her fingers through her long, dark hair. Yes, this was much better.

Glancing at her vintage watch again, she decided she'd better get out there and put the "open" sign on the front door and unlock it. The library was due to open and Mr. Monroe to arrive in less than ten minutes. She quickly left the ladies' room and made her way through the library and museum rooms, stopping briefly, as she did almost every morning, to admire the large portrait of her great Aunt Alexandra that hung prominently in the museum. Prudy did so as a matter of respect for her long-departed great aunt rather than out of obligation or routine. The portrait, no matter the multitude of times she'd admired it, never ceased to amaze her. She smiled at the painting, then walked to the front door, unlocked it and stepped outside into the fresh morning air. It was a beautiful morning. As she hung the "open" sign on the front door, she heard a man's voice calling to her.

"Excuse me, miss. I'm looking for the library and Prudy Trivit."

Prudy slowly turned to face the most handsome man she'd ever seen, at least in person. Tall and broad-shouldered, with a pair of cool, hazel eyes, this fine specimen of manhood was holding two cups of coffee in his hands, staring right at her and smiling. She gulped as she realized this man must be Dylan Monroe. Maybe the gods were smiling upon her today.

"Hello, I'm Prudy Trivit."

"It's a pleasure to meet you, Prudy."

"It's nice to meet you too, Dylan. And thanks for bringing me my morning coffee. I didn't have time to get a cup before I came to work this morning. I'm assuming one of those is mine?" Prudy said with a smile, amazing herself with how cool she was coming off; not showing any of the nervousness she would have thought she'd normally have displayed under the circumstances of meeting such a well-mannered and attractive young man. But this man had immediately put her at ease with his engaging demeanor and friendly smile.

"Oh, yes, of course. Here you are," Dylan said as he carefully handed her the cup of coffee. "Be careful to hold it by the insulated cover so you don't burn yourself. The coffee is really hot."

"Thanks," she said as their hands touched ever so slightly as Prudy took the cup from him, and a twinge of electricity seemed to pass between them. "Let's go into the library where we can sit down and talk."

Dylan opened the door for her and followed her inside. He looked around at the ornate, interior wood moldings and colorful stained glass windows that bejeweled the huge foyer of the mansion that housed the elaborate Mystic Port Museum and Library.

"How fortunate you are to work in such a grand and historic mansion. This place is magnificent. I've only seen such elaborate architecture in books and magazines. You must absolutely love working here."

"Yes, I agree that this place is magnificent. It's the pride of the citizens of Mystic Port, although there is no shortage of historical homes and landmarks in this town. And yes, I really do enjoy my job and working here."

"How long have you worked here."

"It's been almost six years."

"Your specialty is history, isn't it?"

"Yes, American and French history and literature. You're right, there is quite an interesting history held within these walls. Like they say...if walls could talk."

"Do you happen to know if this mansion was once actually someone's home?"

"Yes, this was actually the summer home of a very wealthy family from Boston, the Winthrops. Their family was known as one of the Boston Brahmins, they were the elite upper class families of Boston who were descended from the earliest English colonists."

"Brahmins, I've never heard that term before. Were they just rich or was it like a private club or something?"

"Oh, it was much more than a club. And you had to be more than rich. No new money in this group. These Brahmins, besides coming from a successful family and an elite background, had to be successful in their own right. Most of them headed up an acceptable business or venture that somehow contributed to the wealth of the state of Massachusetts. The ideal Brahmin was the very essence of enlightened aristocracy," she said with the raise of an eyebrow. "He was not only wealthy but was required to display certain acceptable personal virtues and well-bred character traits. The term was coined in 1861 by Oliver Wendell Holmes. Although Holmes used the term to describe Boston's elite upper class, the original Brahmins were the smallest, but most elite social class of the Hindu caste system."

"Were these Boston Brahmins involved in politics or hold positions of power?"

"The Brahmins were often community leaders and would be involved in cultivating the arts, supporting charities, colleges and hospitals. They were definitely the upper crust of Boston. The Brahmin's wielded a strong political influence and played an important role in the cultural development of the City of Boston. Many of the Brahmins were descendants of Massachusetts' earliest founders, the Puritans, and they very much valued the historical significance of the American Revolution."

"So these Winthrops, do you know how long they lived here in this mansion?"

"No, I don't know exactly how many years they lived here. This was their summer residence. I do know that in the early 1900's, after the father, John Winthrop passed away, his son, also named John, inherited the estate. He spent little time here, as his interests, both business and personal, were in Boston. I believe he sold the mansion to the Town of Mystic Port for considerably less than it was actually worth, with the stipulation that it be used as a museum and library. And it has remained that way for over a hundred years."

"That's information I can definitely use in the article. This may sound like a rather strange question, but do you happen to know if the the father passed away here in this mansion?"

"I don't really know, but I could probably find out for you. Is it important?"

"No, not really. I was just being inquisitive. I guess it's just my nature as a journalist. I thought maybe this place might be haunted, which could add a mysterious and intriguing element to the article."

"Really?" Prudy laughed uneasily.

"Have you ever seen what you thought was a ghost here in the mansion?"

"A ghost? No, I can't say I've actually ever seen a ghost here."

"Have you heard any strange noises?"

"Well...this place is old and hearing some strange noises is normal. There's the occasional banging of pipes in the walls and some creaking of the wood floors, but nothing too unusual, considering the age of this place."

Dylan laughed. "So no howling, screaming or the sound of chains being dragged around?"

Prudy laughed nervously. "No, I assure you, nothing as frightening as that."

As they proceeded through the museum to the library, Prudy pointed out paintings and items of historical significance. She stopped in front of the massive portrait of her great aunt. The beautiful, young woman had striking dark hair and intense deep, brown eyes. She was strategically holding an elegant fan in front of her face obscuring her mouth. But one could tell from the gleam in her eyes that she was smiling. The stunningly gorgeous woman was wearing an exquisite gold satin gown. Next to her portrait was another painting of the same woman. This painting featured her standing next to a velvet fainting couch in front of an opulent fireplace, and she was not holding a fan, so you could see her entire face. The beautiful woman seemed to be gazing at someone or something, and she smiled serenely. Dylan appeared to be mesmerized.

"She's impressive, isn't she?"

"Definitely impressive and quite beautiful. Who is she?"

"That is my Great Aunt Alexandra Beaudicort, wife of the mayor of Mystic Port back in the late eighteen hundreds."

"You don't say. She's stunning, Prudy." Dylan looked at the portrait, then back at Prudy. He did this several times.

"I definitely see a resemblance to her when I look at you. You could be sisters, maybe even twins."

Prudy smiled. "Thank you. I'll most definitely take that as a compliment."

"It was definitely meant as a compliment. Beaudicort, that's French, isn't it?"

"Yes, it's French. Her ancestors, and mine, came here from France after the American Revolution ended. It's quite the story about a young couple who met and fell in love on the long voyage from Collioure,

France to Boston Harbor, married and then journeyed here to Mystic Port, settled here and raised a family."

"That is quite interesting. I didn't realize there were many French citizens who came to America at that time, right after the American Revolution. I would have thought most Europeans would have been on the side of England."

"Most were, but not the case with the French. They valued freedom as much as we red-blooded Americans, thus the French Revolution. For example, just take the Marquis de Lafayette, for instance, who actually came here from France to meet George Washington and offer his assistance to the general. Lafayette joined the Continental Army at the young age of seventeen. Can you imagine? He could have done almost anything he wanted, as he was of the nobility. But he chose to come to America to assist General Washington and help us fight for our freedom. He was an invaluable aide to General Washington and extremely loyal. As a matter of fact, Washington and Lafayette shared a close companionship throughout the entire Revolutionary War. Actually, Lafayette spent that awful, harsh winter of 1777-78 with Washington and his men at Valley Forge, suffering through the hardships along with the other soldiers at the encampment."

"I do remember learning in the American history class I took in college that the soldiers encamped at Valley Forge were dealing with awful conditions, including a smallpox epidemic. It must have been a long and horrible winter. I wonder how many soldiers died."

"During the encampment at Valley Forge, an estimated two thousand soldiers died from smallpox. A great many more from malnutrition, frostbite and other dreadful diseases. Something to notate about the smallpox epidemic at Valley Forge is that George Washington recognized the severity of the outbreak and ordered the inoculation of the troops. His decision to inoculate the troops, although considered questionable and quite risky at the time, was thankfully successful. Did you know that was the first time a mass inoculation was conducted in this country? Had Washington not made the decision to inoculate the troops against smallpox, it could have wiped out the entire American fighting force and we could have lost the Revolutionary War."

"It sounds like Washington, besides being a great general, was a visionary. I mean to inoculate an entire fighting force with no assurance whether or not to it would work? That took guts."

"Yes, he was a visionary, as well as a remarkable general and leader."

"Prudy, you certainly are a wealth of historical information. I'm afraid my knowledge of American history is somewhat limited, and my knowledge of French history is even worse. But I am extremely interested in it. Can you tell me more about Layfayette? I knew he was an interesting historical figure, but I wasn't aware he was that young or that he actually served with our military."

"Of course. While serving with our troops, Lafayette was shot in the leg during the Battle of Brandywine. Thousands of troops fought at Brandywine. It was the second longest one day battle of the Revolutionary War with the troops engaged for over eleven hours of continuous fighting. Can you imagine? Lafayette did recover from the gunshot wound and briefly returned to France. He then returned to America once again, this time accompanied by thousands of French troops. Lafayette's troops joined our troops and ultimately helped in forcing the British, who were now seriously outnumbered, to surrender in 1781 at Yorktown, Virginia."

"Do you happen to know what happened to Lafayette after the American Revolution was over? Did he return to France?"

"Yes, after the Revolutionary War ended, Lafayette returned to France and became a prominent leader in the French Revolution. He was appointed as the commander of the Paris National Guard. In 1792, Lafayette was captured by Austrian forces and spent several years in prison. He was later released and he returned to France once again. In 1824, by invitation from President James Monroe, Lafayette toured the United States where he was met appropriately with a hero's welcome. Lafayette died in 1834 at the age of seventy-six and was laid to rest in a large private cemetery in Paris. The soil used at his gravesite was soil from France as well as some soil taken from Bunker Hill, as was his request. An American flag flies over his grave. History has remembered him as a hero of two countries."

"I'll say he was a hero. You certainly do know your facts. I can tell I'm a bit out of my league."

Prudy smiled at him. "Well, I've been studying French and American history for years. It's something I've always taken an interest in. I'm sure you're a much better journalist than I could ever hope to be."

They finally reached the library after stopping to look at several other works of art. They then sat down at a huge, wooden, intricately carved library table.

"You don't mind if I record our interview, do you, Prudy? It's so much easier than taking notes, and much less time-consuming." Dylan asked as he pulled a small recorder from his jacket pocket.

"No, I don't really mind. Just don't let me hear what you've recorded. I so dislike hearing my own voice."

"You know, everyone says that," Dylan said as he smiled at Prudy. "But you have a very nice voice, actually."

Prudy smiled shyly.

Dylan turned on the recorder and started asking questions. "I'm intrigued by this Beaudicort woman. Can you tell me more about her?"

"Yes, well...I can certainly say, and everyone who knows her story would probably agree, that she was an intriguing woman. I doubt there is one inhabitant of Mystic Port that hasn't heard about my notorious Great Aunt Alexandra. Her husband, Samuel Beaudicort, was the mayor of Mystic Port in the eighteen nineties. His bride, Alexandra, was actually in charge of his mayoral campaign. It was quite unusual for a woman prior to women's suffrage to hold a position of such importance, and to have been successful in getting her husband elected."

"I'm curious as to why you described her as intriguing, and you also used the word notorious when describing her."

"I think that will become clear to you after you've heard the entire story about her."

"Well now I am intrigued. It sounds like maybe she was a woman ahead of her time."

"Yes, from what I've been told and from what I've read about her, she was one of those women who worked hard and wanted to have it all: a loving marriage, successful career, children, and she had an extreme interest in politics, which most women at the time did not. Or at least they didn't have the time or support needed to be involved in politics or holding office."

"She must have had a very interesting and full life."

"Oh...I think you could definitely say her life was interesting, but full...no."

Dylan looked concerned. "Why do you say that?"

Prudy sighed. "A murder occurred, followed by what I believe to be a serious miscarriage of justice. She did have one child though, a son named Simon. Unfortunately, before she had a chance to have any more children, her husband, the mayor, died suddenly while in office. Devastated as she was to have lost her husband at such an early age, leaving her a widow at the young age of twenty-four. I have no doubt she would have carried on displaying grace and great strength. I read in the town's historical archives we have here in the library, that she wanted to take her husband's place as mayor, but she was unable to do so."

"Do you mean because she was a woman?"

"I'm not sure if she could have become mayor or not. I rather doubt it. But she wasn't given the chance because unfortunately something happened that changed her life forever." Prudy paused for effect.

"You mean besides losing her husband, there was another traumatic event? What happened to her?"

"Alexandra was arrested for the murder of her husband."

Dylan appeared shocked.

"You mean her husband didn't just die, but he was murdered by his wife, that beautiful woman in the portrait?"

"That has been debated in this town for as long as I can remember. What happened was, Mayor Beaudicort, Alexandra's husband, collapsed after eating lunch in his office with his wife—food she had brought for him to eat."

"What was the cause of death?"

"They said he appeared to have suffered a sudden heart attack."

"And how could they possibly blame Alexandra for her husband having a heart attack?"

"They found pieces of leaves and flower petals from the digitalis plant in the salad Alexandra had brought for him as part of his lunch. They even found some chewed up leaves in his mouth that he was unable to swallow once the digitalis had taken affect."

"Digitalis? Isn't that the drug that's derived from the foxglove plant that's now used as a heart medication?"

"Yes, but digitalis wasn't manufactured as a drug until the twentieth century. In the late eighteen hundreds, American Indians were the only ones actually using digitalis as a medicinal drug. It's very unpredictable, the precise dosage given is of extreme importance. The right amount can assist the function of the heart, slow it down a bit so it doesn't have to work so hard. But too much can cause the heart to slow down dramatically, or even stop functioning completely."

"So the mayor suffered a heart attack because of the digitalis in the foxglove plant he was served in his salad for lunch that day?"

Prudy sighed deeply. "The cause of death was listed as a heart attack, but it was actually more like heart failure. But yes, unfortunately, that's what killed him."

"What's the difference between a heart attack and heart failure?"

"I'm not a doctor, but I believe a heart attack is when the blood flow to the heart is blocked which causes damage to the heart muscle. Heart failure is when the heart slows down too much and just stops functioning. An overdose of digitalis can cause that to happen. It's called digitalis toxicity."

"I see, how awful. What was the date of the mayor's death, for the record?"

"I'll have to look that up for you. I have a copy of Mayor Beaudicort's obituary somewhere here with these papers." Prudy pulled her glasses from her jacket pocket and quickly slipped them on. She shuffled through the papers until she found the record she was looking for.

"Here it is. Samuel Henry Beaudicort died on June 15, 1897."

"Could I see that copy of the obituary?"

"Of course, here you are. Are you looking for something in particular?"

"No, not really. I just wanted to see if there was any additional information on the certificate that might be pertinent."

Dylan quickly perused the copy, then handed it back to her. Prudy removed her glasses and slipped them back into her pocket.

"So they accused his wife of murdering him? I wonder what evidence they had to substantiate arresting her. I mean, her taking his lunch to him sounds circumstantial to me. What actual proof did they have?"

"Other than the fact that Alexandra had taken the salad to him as part of his lunch, and the fact that the authorities found pieces of chewed up foxglove leaves in his mouth, I don't think they had any actual proof. But they did arrest her. Alexandra swore she loved her husband, was devastated by his death, and her defense was that although she had taken her husband's lunch to him that day, she hadn't actually prepared the salad."

"Well then, who did?"

"She accused her housekeeper, a woman by the name of Amelia Sanderson, of the murder of her husband. Alexandra told the authorities that Amelia had prepared the mayor's lunch that day, as she did every day, and that she, Alexandra, had merely taken it to him. She reportedly told authorities that her husband was having his lunch and she

32

had stayed, as she usually did, to keep him company during his lunch hour. Alexandra said he suddenly slumped over at his desk and then fell from his chair onto the floor. His secretary in the adjoining room, reported that she heard Alexandra screaming for help. By the time the authorities arrived, he was dead."

"I guess they didn't believe Alexandra when she told them she hadn't prepared the salad."

"No, unfortunately I guess they didn't. Amelia, the housekeeper, told the police she had prepared the mayor's lunch that day, everything except for the salad. She told the authorities that Alexandra had insisted on making the salad that day herself. You see, Alexandra was an avid gardener, always growing things, including vegetables. She was always pruning and watering her plants and taking good care of her gardens. Besides her prize-winning roses, foxgloves were among her favorites. When the authorities investigated in the gardens, besides lettuce leaves in the vegetable garden being torn off, which is something you'd expect in a salad, several of the foxglove plants had tears in the leaves and had flowers plucked off. Amelia swore she didn't even know what a foxglove plant looked like. I guess they believed her because they arrested Alexandra."

"But certainly there was a trial, right?"

"Well yes, there was trial."

"Was Alexandra convicted of murdering her husband?"

"No, she was never actually convicted."

"Well that's good."

"Just wait until you hear the rest of the story."

Chapter Two

Dylan leaned back in his chair and stretched, then switched off the recorder, took a deep breath, and released it slowly. He smiled at Prudy.

"This is a really intriguing story, one that I think will make for an interesting article. But I can tell this interview with you is going to require a lot more time than I initially thought. How about we take a break and go get another cup of coffee?"

"That sounds like a good idea, Dylan. I could use another cup, but I can't leave the library until my assistant, Tina, comes in at ten, which is in about fifteen minutes. But we can take another walk around the museum, if you'd like to stretch your legs."

"Yes, that sounds like a good idea, and I'd especially like to take another look at the portrait of Alexandra."

"Why Mr. Monroe, I do believe you might have a crush on my dear departed aunt. Could that be?"

Dylan laughed. "Perhaps, I am intrigued with the story and rather captivated by the painting itself, but even more so with the undeniable similarities between you and her.

I'm serious, you could be twins. But I'm sure you've been told that many times before. I mean the resemblance is undeniable. Certainly other people have told you that."

"Oh sure, people who see the portrait often remark about the resemblance. And even I think there is a resemblance myself. But I think you should wait to decide how you really feel about her until after you've heard the rest of the story. I mean you may be falling for a suspected murderer, Dylan."

"I'm shaking in my boots," Dylan said with a grin. "Seriously though, I have a hard time believing that someone as beautiful as Alexandra could actually be a murderer."

"I agree, and I really don't think Alexandra was the murderer."

"Do you believe Amelia committed the murder?"

"Yes, I believe so. But like I said, you'll have to decide for yourself until after you've heard the rest of the story."

"I hope that will be soon because I'm definitely intrigued."

"Don't worry, I won't string you along for any longer than it takes to go get coffee before I tell you the rest of the story."

They both rose from their seats at the library table and walked towards the museum. Just outside the open doorway to the museum, both Prudy and Dylan stopped dead in their tracks. A cold pocket of air blew out from the museum and they could hear what sounded like a strong, howling wind blowing through the room. Loose papers and debris were being pushed out towards them into the library, the wind blowing Prudy's hair all about, snaking strands across her face, making it hard for her to see. Then the lights started flickering on and off. Suddenly, there was a loud banging noise coming from in the museum, like someone was pounding on the walls. The lights continued to flicker on and off, causing Prudy to become disoriented. She did not attempt to move from where she was standing for fear she'd fall.

"What the hell?" Dylan yelled as he moved towards the museum but was sidelined when a pencil tore through the air and hit him squarely in the forehead. "Ouch!"

"Are you alright, Dylan?" Prudy yelled with panic in her voice.

"Yes, but an airborne pencil just missed hitting me in the eyes," he yelled back. "It looks like someone must have come in before and left the door open, but I didn't realize it was supposed to be stormy this morning. I mean it was perfectly clear just an hour ago."

"Me either. I had no idea we were supposed to get hit with storms this morning," Prudy shouted back loudly so he'd be able to hear her above all the commotion. "Do you think you can get in there and shut the door to the outside?"

"Yes, I think so. But you stay here, Prudy."

"I will but please be careful."

"Don't worry. It's just a storm and some wind."

Dylan made his way into the museum, and as soon as he got through the open doorway and stepped into the room, the wind totally stopped blowing. Papers and debris seemed to hang in mid air, and then suddenly plummeted to the floor. Out of the corner of his eye, Dylan could see what appeared to be the outline of a shimmering figure as it dissipated into the air. "What the...?" He rationalized that it must have been the light from a prism, as sunlight streamed in through the window. The pounding noise had stopped and the lights were no longer flickering on and off. Dylan knew something quite strange had just happened because the front door was not even open. Where did all that wind come from if not from outside?

"Dylan?" Prudy slowly entered the room. "Oh my goodness, just look at this mess. Thanks for shutting the door. I wonder who came in and then left it open. Maybe Tina who was carrying a box of books or something, and then she went back outside to get more boxes...except...I don't see any boxes. Maybe she forgot her phone or something and went back out to her car to get it. It looks like the storm must be over. That was quick."

Just then the door flew open and Tina the library assistant walked in. She stopped dead in her tracks and starred, first at Prudy, then at Dylan, and back at Prudy again.

"Oh my goodness, Tina. Did you just drive here through that awful storm? You don't look any worse for the wear. You're not even wet."

Snapping her gum like a high school drama queen, Tina replied, "Ah, what storm, Pru?"

Dylan and Prudy shot bewildered sideways glances at each other.

"Prudy, aren't you going to introduce me to your friend?"

"Oh, sorry, the storm frazzled my nerves. Dylan Monroe, this is Tina Thomas, my assistant. Tina works here part-time. She's also enrolled in college but has the summer off from classes."

Dylan extended his hand to Tina, who optimistically shook it and smiled broadly. Tina, only nineteen and a bit immature, was obviously taken with Dylan's good looks. She then turned to stare at Prudy again and said, "New hairstyle you got going there, Pru? What do you call that, the wind blown look?"

"Oh...no," Prudy said, laughing nervously, "No, when you left the door open and the wind from the storm came tearing through into the library, it made a terrible mess of my hair, not to mention these papers all over the place, and anything else that wasn't locked down."

Tina looked at them quizzically.

"Storm? Wind? What are you talking about? Have you two been drinking or something?"

Prudy, rather perturbed and embarrassed by Tina's question quite abruptly replied, "Of course not!"

Dylan interjected. "The only thing we were drinking was coffee."

"And what's this storm and wind you keep talking about?"

Dylan interrupted, "Prudy, the front door wasn't open when I came in here."

"What? Tina, did you come in before, leave the door open, and then go back outside to get something and now just come back in again?"

"What are you talking about? Okay, this is a joke, right? You're playing with me now, right?"

"No, this is definitely not a joke and what just happened here is all rather strange and extremely disconcerting. I'm just trying to make some sense out of it. Tina, seriously now, wasn't there a really bad storm that passed through with strong winds that ended just a few minutes ago?"

Tina snapped her gum again and laughed. "Seriously, no. There was no wind, no rain, not even cloudy really."

Prudy was stunned. "And you just got here for the first time when you came in a minute ago?"

"Yes, I just got here, walked in, and to be honest, I thought I caught you two in the middle of something, what with your hair down and all disheveled, papers everywhere on the floor, and Dylan here looking like the cat who swallowed the canary."

Dylan snapped to his defense. "This look is total bewilderment at what just happened here."

Tina adamantly asked again, "Would someone please tell me exactly what you're talking about?"

Prudy, rather exasperated at this point combed her fingers through her tangled hair, walked over to the door and peered through the side window panels, totally astonished with the fact that the weather was fair, not a cloud in the sky, the sun shining brightly, and there were no raindrops on the glass of the windows. "I'm not sure what happened here, but I will tell you this; something definitely did happen, something very strange indeed."

Tiny snapped her gum again. "And you say that because why?"

Prudy sighed in frustration and then tried to explain the scenario to Tina, who strained to keep herself from laughing out loud because she assumed Prudy was just telling her this crazy made up story to conceal the fact she and Dylan had in fact been fooling around. She shook her head, and finally unable to contain herself any longer, laughed out loud. Prudy gave her a stern look.

"Well, I guess I better clean up this mess," Tina said with a note of sarcasm in her voice.

"Yes, thanks, please do. Also, would you please put the new books that came in on the shelves? I've already entered them in inventory on the computer and they are stamped inside. Make sure you put them in the right places on the shelves this time so people can find the book they're looking for in the right place. Mrs. Latimer had a fit last week because she couldn't find the book she was looking for. Turns out it was a cozy mystery but it was shelved in the thriller section."

"Yes, ma'am!" She snapped her gum again.

"And Tina, get rid of the gum! Dylan and I are going to the Brew Awhile for some coffee."

"Okay, but you better drive carefully, and beware of sudden storms and bad weather," Tina yelled after them. "You never know when one of those crazy storms could pop up and all hell could break loose."

Dylan turned to grimace at Tina, then opened the door for Prudy, and they stepped out into the bright sunshine of a beautiful, late summer day, not a cloud in the sky and just a light, gentle breeze.

"Prudy, I am totally freaked out by what just happened in there. I think what I witnessed in the museum might have been something supernatural or paranormal."

"Paranormal, you mean like ghosts or something?"

"Well...yeah. How else would you explain what just happened in there? You know, I saw something pretty strange when I first walked into the museum room."

"Strange? Tell me, exactly what did you see? Can you describe it?"

"I'm not sure exactly. The best way I can describe it is, it was like this weird form that looked something like ice crystals floating in the air, but kind of in the shape of a figure. When I looked directly at it, it disappeared. It seemed to just dissipate into thin air. I thought it might have been sunlight streaming in through rain and clouds outside, but obviously there was no rain, no wind, and no storm. Another weird thing was, when I stepped into the room, the wind suddenly stopped, like whoever or whatever was causing the disturbance didn't want to be caught in the act."

"You said it had a form. Do you mean like a human form?"

"I only saw it for maybe two or three seconds before it disappeared, but yes, I believe it looked like a human form."

"Was it a male or female form?"

"I really couldn't tell. It disappeared so quickly."

Prudy stared at Dylan and her voice stuck in her throat as she tried to make some sense of the situation. "I can't explain it. I've never encountered anything quite like that before. I mean I didn't see what you saw. But I did witness feeling that pocket of very cold air, and the wind and the papers blowing all around, and the lights flickering on and off. Not to mention that terrible banging noise. What was that? At the time, I thought someone had come in and left the door open and that there had been a bad storm with wind. But there was no storm."

Dylan opened the passenger door of his car and Prudy got in. He then walked around the back of the car and got in the driver's side.

Prudy opened the visor mirror and looked at herself. "Goodness, I look like a goblin myself."

Dylan smiled at her. "But a very attractive goblin."

Prudy smiled shyly. She then pulled a brush from her purse and quickly brushed her hair. Both of them were still thinking about what had happened, and at first, neither spoke as they drove into the center of town. Dylan parked near the historic town square, where a large statue of Nathanael Greene, a local general in the Continental Army, stood proudly.

"That is one really large statue. Who is it? Must be somebody important."

"That's Nathanael Greene, who was commissioned as a brigadier general commanding three regiments who served with Washington's army in Boston. He became one of Washington's most trusted generals."

"I guess he was from this area?"

"Yes, he was born near here in Potowomut, Rhode Island."

"Potowomut, that's a funny name."

"It translates to "land of fires" which is the Narragansett Indian name for peninsula."

"Your knowledge of the local history amazes me almost as much as your knowledge of American and French history."

Prudy smiled at him.

Dylan put the car in park and turned off the ignition but made no attempt to get out of the car. Instead, he just sat there, deep in thought. He noticed that Prudy glanced at him but she said nothing. She too was obviously deep in thought, trying to make some sense of what had happened in the museum.

He finally broke the silence. "I can't stop thinking about what happened. I'm still freaked out, are you?"

"Oh yes, most definitely. I am totally freaked out. What I witnessed in there is not something I think I'll soon forget, if ever."

"What do you think we should do about what happened, Prudy?"

"Do? Well, what can we do? I mean we could try to pretend it didn't happen, or just accept it as some strange phenomenon, one of those unexplainable things that happen sometimes, and let it go. But like I said, I don't think I'll be able to forget about it any time soon. Probably never. Or...maybe we could conduct an investigation," she said, with the raise of one eyebrow and a twinkling in her eyes.

It was easy for Dylan to determine from Prudy's expression, and from the inflection in her voice, what Prudy wanted to do. He was glad she wanted to investigate what had happened, as he was intrigued, both with the phenomenon that had occurred but also very much with Prudy herself. She had an inquisitive nature, like himself. He nodded in approval.

"Investigate, huh? But how would we investigate? I don't have a clue where we'd start or what we would do."

"I'm not sure either. Maybe we'd have to look into what ghost hunters do."

"But they have all that special equipment they use, like cameras that actually detect the presence of a spirit or spirits. Do you know of anyone who has experience with hunting ghosts?"

Prudy laughed. "No, not in Mystic Port. There are several psychics residing in the area, but I think you actually have to be a psychic medium to be able to have contact with spirits. My Aunt Maggie, who is also descended from Alexandra, by the way, is a bit psychic, and she believes in ghosts or spirits."

"You don't say. I'd like to meet her if possible. I've never met a psychic in person before. So you think what I saw was a ghost or spirit?"

"I didn't say that. But I wouldn't rule it out either. If you had just seen that apparition, or whatever it was, and none of the other strange things had happened, I would think it was just some weird formation of dust particles appearing in the sunlight streaming in the windows or something. But all the other things that happened; the extreme cold, the intensity of the wind, papers blowing everywhere, the lights flickering on and off, well it adds up to something supernatural, that's for sure. I mean there is no other explanation is there?. How does wind suddenly start blowing through a room if it's not coming in from outside? Why did the temperature drop so dramatically? And that horrifically loud banging. That's not natural, so it must be supernatural, right?"

"I guess that is a legitimate assumption. Maybe I can do some research and read up on hauntings, see if there's any accounts of hauntings similar to what we witnessed. There are accounts all over the internet of ghost sightings. I must say, this has been an extremely interesting morning so far. So what happens next?" What should we do?"

"We'll have to discuss it further. But first things first. I could really use another cup of coffee."

"Yeah, me too. Let's go."

Chapter Three

The Brew Awhile Coffee House was in what had once been, in its day, a very upscale Victorian clothing shop, whose gingerbread millwork was now painted a shameful duet of funky pink and a nasty shade of purple. Dylan, gentleman that he was, opened the passenger side car door for Prudy. The couple walked the few short steps to the coffee house and stopped to look at the blackboard sign outside the entrance showing the specials of the day.

"The Frothy Frog's Brew sounds interesting, doesn't it?" Dylan asked, amused.

Prudy laughed, "Call me boring, but I think I'll just get my basic black."

"You are anything but boring, Prudy."

Once inside, the intoxicating aroma of freshly brewed coffee enticed their senses. Both Prudy and Dylan each got plain black coffee and sat down at one of the small round tables near a window towards the back of the shop.

Although it was mid-August, and the weather was still quite warm, Prudy shivered from a chill she got just thinking about that pocket of cold air that felt like it had encased her in the library. She placed her ice-cold hands around her hot cup of coffee, letting the warmth permeate through her fingers. She looked up and smiled at Dylan, who momentarily appeared like he was far off somewhere else, probably still analyzing recent events. Prudy's cell phone vibrated in her suit jacket pocket. She pulled it out and saw that the call was from her Aunt Maggie.

"Hello, Aunt Maggie."

"Hello, sweetie. How's it going? Listen, I'm on pins and needles here, so tell me, how did the interview go with that journalist from The Coastal Press?"

"It's been a very interesting conversation so far, but we got a bit interrupted and will have to continue the interview later. I was telling Mr. Monroe the story about Alexandra and the mayor's murder. Actually, I'm having coffee with him at the Brew Awhile right now."

"Oh how nice, dear. If he's interested in the story about the mayor's murder, did you happen to mention to him that we live in the mayor's and Alexandra's house? Maybe he'd like a tour of the house."

"No, I didn't mention that to him, but I will. I think Mr. Monroe would be very interested in seeing the house where Alexandra lived," Prudy said as she threw an inquisitive glance at Dylan.

Dylan's eyes widened and he shook his head vigorously in the affirmative.

"I have a supper idea. Why don't you ask him to have dinner here with us this evening? That way he can see the house where Alexandra lived and maybe see some of her belongings, if he's interested."

"That's a great idea, because as it happens, he wants to meet you and we need your advice about something anyway."

"Oh really, my advice, about what dear?"

"Let's just say some rather strange things occurred at the museum today. Things that we think were probably supernatural occurrences. But we'll fill you in at dinner tonight."

"I can't stand the suspense. Can you just tell me, does it have anything to do with Alexandra's portrait?"

"Yes, I think it might. I believe Alexandra could be trying to tell us something. Dylan saw what he thinks might be a ghost or spirit, and from the velocity of the energy exhibited, I believe it may have possibly been Alexandra. Thankfully, no one was hurt and there was no real damage."

"Really? I'm looking forward to hearing about it. We'll talk more at dinner. I think I'll make my famous seafood bouillabaisse."

"That would be wonderful. I think Mr. Monroe probably likes seafood."

Dylan nodded again, vigorously.

"Yes, he does like seafood."

"Great, I can't wait to meet him."

"He's eager to meet you too. See you later then. Goodbye, Aunt Maggie."

Dylan had a look of extreme intrigue on his face, but waited for Prudy to fill him in. Prudy smiled coyly at him but said nothing. Dylan leaned in closer to her.

"Are you going to just keep me in suspense about what you were discussing with your aunt? I'm kind of on the edge of my seat here. I could only hear your end of the conversation. You mentioned thinking what happened at the museum may have been the spirit of Alexandra?"

"I'm just trying to put my thoughts together. I wasn't sure I wanted to involve someone else in a situation that I thought was probably all but dead, if you'll excuse the pun."

"What situation? What are you talking about?"

Prudy continued. "Alexandra mysteriously died in prison. This was during the trial to determine her guilt or innocence when she was accused of the murder of her husband, the mayor."

"Alexandra died? How did she die? What happened to her?"

"No one knows for sure exactly what happened. It's a bit of a mystery. One that quite a few people, including myself, have been trying to solve for years, But I'll tell you what I do know. One morning during the trial, the bailiff went to her cell to escort Alexandra to the courtroom, and he found her lying in a heap on the floor. She wasn't breathing. She was dead.

"Go on, please," Dylan pleaded.

"Her cousin, Isabella, with whom Alexandra had been close, circulated a story. Alexandra was convinced her housekeeper, Amelia Sanderson, was responsible for Samuel Beaudicort's untimely demise. Supposedly, Amelia was the one who prepared his lunch that day and every day. It was one of her duties. But she claimed she hadn't made the salad. Alexandra contended that Amelia prepared the entire lunch, including the salad just as she did every day. After all, why would she, Alexandra, prepare only part of the lunch for her husband just this one time? That made no sense. We believe she was getting close to finding out the truth about Amelia, both that she had poisoned the mayor, and that she had possibly murdered before. Isabella swore that Amelia also poisoned Alexandra, to keep her from exposing the truth about her during the trial."

"Wow, that's quite a story. Did you say Isabella thought Amelia had possibly murdered someone before the mayor?"

"Yes, I guess Isabella was doing a bit of an investigation regarding Amelia's past, specifically her past employers. What she found out put a whole different light on the mayor's murder."

"What did Isabella find out?"

"As the story goes, she discovered that the husband of the woman Amelia worked for before she went to work for the

Beaudicort's, had mysteriously and suddenly taken ill and died."

"Don't tell me. Let me guess. Sudden heart failure?"

"That's what was listed as the cause of death by the coroner on the death certificate."

"You're right, that sure does put a whole new light on things. Just the fact that Alexandra was murdered in prison while awaiting trial makes you think it was to silence her. Knowing Amelia was suspected of probably murdering her previous employer, makes me think she did indeed murder the mayor. It would fit her MO. But what does all of that history have to do with what happened today in the museum?"

"There have been several incidents over the years involving hauntings at my Aunt Maggie's house, where I live also, as well as some strange occurrences at the library and museum."

"Do you mean like what happened this morning?"

"Yes, as far as the museum is concerned, similar to what happened today, but no one ever saw that supernatural form you described. There was just that feeling of hitting a pocket of cold air and occasionally there have been some electrical malfunctions. That's why I looked apprehensive when you asked me if I'd ever seen what I thought was a ghost at the museum."

"Right, and you said you had actually never seen a ghost there. But you didn't mention that you suspected supernatural activity."

"Well, nothing that I'd consider to possibly be supernatural activity has occurred at the museum in a year or two, until today. And at the house, there have been several small fires, things disappearing, strange noises, that sort of thing."

"I wonder why this supernatural activity at the museum started up today."

"It could be that all that discussion we were having about Alexandra and the mayor's murder awoke something that was never really put to rest."

"I understand what you're saying. Can you explain to me what a haunting is?"

"Well, here's just one example. On the 75th anniversary of his death, there was an article in the local newspaper about how Samuel Beaudicort was murdered by his wife, Alexandra. My aunt was a young woman at the time and was intrigued with the article and the whole story behind the mayor's demise, and how his beautiful, young wife had been suspected of being the murderer. She kept the newspaper with the article, put it away in a drawer and then forgot about it. A few years ago, she was cleaning out the drawer, found the newspaper with the article and pulled it out for me to read. I read the article and left the newspaper on the coffee table, then I went to work. Aunt Maggie called me at work later that day and told me there had been a small fire at the house. There was some minor smoke damage, but nothing too serious. However, the newspaper was found totally burned and was the cause of the fire. I think when a spirit, or ghost if you will, does things to get your attention, that's a haunting."

"Oh...I see. So do you think Alexandra was mad about the article in the newspaper portraying her as the murderer, and she was trying to make a statement?"

"Yes, that's exactly what we think. And that's just one example. There were a few, thankfully small fires, electrical malfunctions, personal items disappearing, and strange noises being heard over the years. At one point last summer, things were getting so weird that Aunt Maggie decided to call in a poltergeist interventionist."

"What exactly is a poltergeist?"

"A poltergeist is when a ghost or spirit continually does things to get your attention, similar to a haunting, like moving furniture, banging things, removing objects, causing a disturbance, that sort of thing."

"And maybe like setting a fire?"

"Yes, and that was just the beginning."

"It sounds to me like a poltergeist might occur if a spirit is very angry and it could be more dangerous than a haunting."

"Yes, I think that's probably true."

"Was the poltergeist interventionist able to help?"

"Not really. He said he felt that we were indeed dealing with an active spirit. Well, we were pretty sure of that anyway. His only suggestion was that we be careful not to instigate any attention, if at all possible. I do have to admit though, things have settled down at the house since his visit last summer."

Dylan finished his coffee and sat back in his chair. He studied Prudy who looked up and smiled at him.

"Dylan, I better get back to the library before Tina gets into trouble."

"Sure, I understand. I can imagine she's a bit of a handful, that one. A real trouble maker. I have to get going myself anyway."

"Can you come to the house at about 6:30 tonight?"

"Oh, I'll be there. You can bet money on it. What's the address?"

"It's on Beaudecort Boulevard, number 412. Beaudicort is the street that runs parallel below Main Street."

"Beaudicort Boulevard, I'll remember that for sure. I'll be there at 6:30. I'm anxious to see the house, meet your aunt, and to continue the interview. Come on, I'll drive you back to the library."

Chapter Four

Prudy stood at the kitchen sink gazing out the back window at the beautiful gardens that she and her aunt maintained, as she washed the lettuce and cucumbers she would use in the salad she was preparing. Her aunt had dinner baking in the oven.

"I hope your friend likes lasagna, dear."

"Aunt Maggie, who wouldn't like your famous lasagna?"

"Well dear, you never know. I was going to make my famous seafood bouillabaisse, but I couldn't get to the grocery to buy the necessary ingredients I needed."

Prudy turned to face her aunt with a look of concern.

"Why couldn't you get to the grocery store?"

"The damn battery, excuse my French, in that hunk of junk pick-up truck must be dead. I think I might call your cousin Phil and ask him to steal the piece of junk and push it over a cliff." Her aunt winked at her. "Seriously though, I'm tired of spending money to get it fixed, only to have something else go wrong with it. I'm thinking it's getting to the point of not being worth it, if you know what I mean."

Prudy dried her hands off and slowly moved over to stand behind her aunt. "You know, you have more than enough money saved to buy yourself a new car, Aunt Maggie. One that you could rely on."

"Well, I was thinking about that, and then the thought crossed my mind that maybe I should think about giving up my license anyway. I'm well into my eighties now. Continuing to drive at my age just doesn't seem like a very good or responsible thing to do. What do you think I should do, Prudy?"

Prudy slowly sat down at the kitchen table and motioned for her aunt to sit as well.

"I think you should do what you would be comfortable with and what you think would be best for you. I certainly wouldn't mind doing the grocery shopping or driving you anywhere you might need to go, but I want you to be sure. Your happiness is important to me, but so is your safety."

"You're such a wonderful niece, my dear, dear Prudy. I appreciate your concern for me, and you've made it easy for me to make a decision. I just made up my mind, I'm going to stop driving. I don't feel comfortable behind the wheel anymore."

"Okay. We'll see if Phil wants the truck. If not, we'll have it junked."

Maggie sighed in relief.

"I'm glad that's settled. It's been on my mind for quite a while now."

Prudy rose from her chair at the table and bent to kiss her aunt's cheek. "I'm glad too. Now, I'd better finish making the salad. Dylan will be here soon."

"Oh, here dear. I picked these tomatoes from the garden this afternoon. Put these in your salad."

Prudy finished making the salad and then set the dining room table for three. "I'm going out to the garden to cut a few flowers to put in the vase for the table. I'll be right back, Auntie."

As she walked past the notorious foxglove plants that lined the garden that ran along the side of the house, Prudy laughed to herself, wondering how many times Alexandra had walked this exact same path, past the foxgloves on her way to the rose garden. Of course, these were not the same foxgloves that her Great Aunt Alexandra had planted, but they were in the same garden and in the same location. Prudy and her Aunt Maggie knew this because they had seen the original architectural blueprint of the gardens in an old book they'd found in the attic years earlier. The gardens were usually a topic of conversation for anyone passing by, and the story of Alexandra, the murder of her husband, the mayor, the trial, and the tragic death of Alexandra herself, were kept alive and continued to intrigue many of the townspeople. Prudy had heard these stories most of her life, and there were some townspeople who actually disliked her and her aunt because they believed Alexandra did indeed murder her husband. In her heart, Prudy was convinced that was not true.

As Prudy cut some roses she thought of Dylan, who would be there soon to join her and her aunt for dinner. It was funny that she had known him for less than a day and already felt completely comfortable with him. And he was so handsome and nice. A smile came to her face as she daydreamed about the possibilities.

"Ouch!" A thorn pierced through the tender skin of the flesh in between Prudy's thumb and index finger on her left hand. "Son of a gun," she said as she accidentally smeared bright red blood on her white blouse. She pulled a tissue out of her pocket and held it firmly over the injury. Once she was sure the bleeding had stopped, she continued cutting the roses. She walked back to the foxglove garden and cut a long stem with beautiful pale pink blooms. She then took it with the roses back into the house, filled a large vase with water and placed the foxglove in the middle and surrounded it with the roses. She took a step back and admired her arrangement.

"There, do you like my arrangement of the flowers, Aunt Maggie?"

"Oh, the arrangement is lovely dear. You are so very much like your mother. She used to make lovely arrangements herself. She had a flair for it, you know. I see you do as well. A green thumb and caring for these beautiful gardens must run in the family. We know that Alex loved gardening, as did your mom, and I do also."

Maggie saw the blood on Prudy's blouse. "Did you cut yourself, dear?"

"A thorn from a rose bush jumped out and stabbed me. Nothing that hasn't happened about a hundred times before."

"Here, let's wet a paper towel and get that blood out of your blouse before it sets in."

Maggie blotted the blood stained fabric with the wet paper towel.

"There, it's all out. So, tell me, does Dylan know the story about the foxglove and the salad that supposedly killed the mayor?"

"Oh yes, I told him the story, and he is totally intrigued. Which makes me think that perhaps serving a salad tonight and having a flower arrangement with foxglove in it on the same table might not be such a good idea."

"Ha!" Aunt Maggie laughed. "Yes, you don't want poor Dylan thinking you're trying to murder him!"

Just then there was a knock at the front door. Prudy looked at her watch. "Right on time. It must be Dylan."

Prudy went to the front door and opened it to find Dylan standing there with his arms full of papers and he was also holding a bottle of wine. Prudy looked at him quizzically. Dylan smiled enthusiastically.

"What are all those?"

"I brought some copies of original newspaper articles about the mayor's murder, Alexandra's arrest, and the trial. I did some research online this afternoon after we parted company. I'll tell you about it later. Oh, and I brought you and your aunt a bottle of wine. It's a Merlot. I hope you'll like it. I wasn't sure what went with seafood bouillabaisse."

"Well, as it turns out, my aunt ended up making lasagna which the Merlot will go with perfectly. Thanks so much, Dylan."

"Of course, I'm grateful for the invitation to dinner."

Just then, Aunt Maggie entered the room. To Dylan's astonishment, he noticed that Prudy's aunt had that same look about her eyes as Alexandra had in the portrait, which was the same look he had noticed about Prudy's eyes. That look had captivated him.

"Dylan, this is my Aunt Magnolia, but we call her Maggie."

Dylan handed the bottle of wine to Prudy and then offered to shake hands with her aunt. Maggie smiled and put out her hand, which Dylan gently held for just a moment. After all, she was an older lady and shaking her hand, like she was a business acquaintance, just didn't feel right.

"It's a pleasure to meet another relative of the beautiful and notorious Alexandra Beaudicort. The resemblance is undeniable."

"Well thank you. I will definitely take that as a compliment, Dylan."

He laughed a bit and said, "That's funny, that's exactly what Prudy said."

"The large portrait of her in the museum is stunning, isn't it?"

"Yes, it is, almost magical, definitely captivating. The way she's holding that fan over her mouth so you can't see her expression, but then if you look at her face it's as if her eyes are smiling."

"Smiling eyes, yes, I believe you're right, Dylan. And in the other painting next to the portrait, you can see how truly stunning the gold gown she's wearing really is, because you can see the whole thing."

"Yes, Alexandra looks beautiful in that gown. There's no question about that."

"I understand you're writing an article about the history of Mystic Port for the 250th anniversary and celebration of the town."

"Yes, I am, and with my discovery of this wonderful story that Prudy told me this morning, I think I found the perfect subject matter."

"It all sounds fascinating, and we'll have to discuss this more while we have dinner. But the lasagna is not ready yet, so maybe now would be a good time to give Dylan a tour of the house, Prudy. I'd start with the gardens."

"I'd love a tour of the gardens and this amazing house," Dylan said enthusiastically.

"Sure, let's go out to the yard and I'll show you the foxglove garden."

"You mean Alexandra's foxglove plants are still out there?"

"Well, they're not the same plants, of course, but they're in the exact same location as hers were. As a matter of fact, the gardens are pretty much laid out exactly the same as Alexandra had them originally."

"Really? How do you know that?"

"Aunt Maggie and I have the original blueprints for the gardens. We found them in the attic years ago. Dylan, you can just leave those copies of the newspaper articles here on the coffee table for now. We'll take a look at them after dinner, although I think I've probably seen them all before."

Dylan put the pile of papers down on the coffee table

After stopping to see the foxgloves first, Prudy showed Dylan all around the yard and gardens.

"This is a huge yard, and the gardens are so well cared for. Do you and your aunt take care of the gardening yourselves?"

"We're out here working in the garden a lot, but my cousin, Phil, has a landscaping business and he helps us out. Let's go back inside and I'll show you the house."

Prudy gave Dylan a tour of all the rooms in the house with the exception of the dining room, the kitchen, and the basement. Aunt

Maggie announced that the lasagna was finally finished.

"It would have been done an hour ago if I had turned the oven on! It's a good thing I checked it when you came back in from the yard."

Everyone had a good laugh.

"I'm sure it will be worth the wait, Aunt Maggie."

"It certainly smells delicious." Dylan added.

"Why don't you two go into the dining room, be seated, and I'll serve dinner and then we can have an interesting discussion about the house and the mystery of the Beaudicort murders." Aunt Maggie said with a gleam in her eye.

Dylan followed Prudy into the dining room. He was delighted to see not just one, but two portraits of Alexandra hanging in the dining room, both in beautifully gilded frames. The portraits hung regally side by side over the fireplace. Although they were not as formal or massive as the ones in the museum, they still had Dylan spellbound. He stood in front of the paintings and looked from each one, then at Prudy, noticing even more now, the undeniable likeness between the two women. Except for the modern clothing and Prudy's gorgeous hair being completely down and cascading over her shoulders, he could have been looking at the same person.

A serious look came upon his face as he continued to closely examine the one portrait.

"Prudy, in this portrait, Alexandra looks very serious and is wearing all black in what appears to be mourning attire. Do you know anything about this particular portrait?"

"No, I don't really. Aunt Maggie might know something about it." She turned to look at her aunt.

"I don't know the details about that particular portrait. But I do know that it was customary for a family to sometimes request a portrait of surviving family members after the death of a loved one. Maybe it was after the death of her mother or another close relative. It certainly wasn't after her husband's death because we know she was arrested and incarcerated almost immediately after the murder occurred. There was certainly no time to have a portrait done."

Prudy shook her head. "I can only imagine how frightened and alone she felt. Poor Aunt Alexandra. She lost her husband and her freedom, and then soon, her own life."

Dylan inquired, "Do the townspeople here know that Alexandra was probably murdered while she was imprisoned?"

Prudy explained that many of the people in Mystic Port believed that Alexandra took her own life while she was incarcerated because she had indeed murdered her husband and she was probably quite sure she'd be convicted.

"I'm surprised they didn't investigate to find out Alexandra's cause of death."

Maggie quickly interjected, "I'm not surprised. You might think I'm biased, but I think Amelia paid off the authorities to announce to the general public that Alexandra had killed herself. Amelia had a rather questionable reputation, known for blackmailing wealthy families and bribing local government officials. At least that's what's been rumored for many years."

Prudy shook her head. "The mayor's murder and the cause of Alexandra's death have been debated in this town for probably the last century and most likely will be for many years to come."

Dylan interjected, "Wouldn't you like to find out the whole truth once and for all?"

"Don't think we haven't tried."

Chapter Five

Aunt Maggie, Prudy, and Dylan had finished eating dinner but were still seated at the dining room table, finishing the fine Merlot that Dylan brought along. The wine had them feeling warm and mellow, and Aunt Maggie, downright giddy. The conversation was jovial and there were frequent bouts of laughter.

Despite the jovial conversation and atmosphere, Prudy's mind was still on her Aunt Alexandra, Dylan's interview, and the strange recent occurrence at the museum. "Dylan, is it your intention to try to find out the truth about Mayor Beaudecort's murder?"

"You said you have been investigating about the mayor's murder for quite a long time. The article has to be finished a week before the town's anniversary, so there's limited time to investigate. As far as the article is concerned, I could focus on the history of the town. You've certainly given me a lot to work with already. But personally, I'm intrigued with the murder mystery. I'd like to help you investigate."

"Of course I'd like to be able to prove Alexandra's innocence, but every time we investigate, something, or someone gets in the way. I was rather convinced that I'd reached a dead end with my investigation about the murder of the mayor about a year ago. So, I'd pretty much given up on doing any more research, until today."

"Until this morning, I would have said the idea of a spirit trying to influence someone about something that happened over a hundred years ago was absolutely preposterous. But now, well I'm not sure what to think. I'd like to at least try to help you find out the truth, what really happened and who murdered the mayor, but if it becomes impossible, I'll settle for leaving that question unanswered as far as the article is concerned. There may not be any conclusion about Alexandra's guilt or innocence, but at least the article will pique some more interest in the town's anniversary."

Prudy sat back in her chair, deep in thought, a faraway look in her eyes, when suddenly, her expression changed dramatically.

"What is it, Prudy?" Dylan questioned her, concerned.

"I smell something burning!"

The three of them quickly arose from their chairs and ran into the living room where, to their astonishment, the pile of newspaper copies Dylan had left on the coffee table were starting to smolder; orange embers glowing in the now darkened room. He quickly picked up the pile of papers and yelled for Prudy to open the front door, which she raced to do. Dylan quickly took the papers outside to the front yard and stomped on them until he was sure the smoldering fire was out. He then brought them back inside and examined them. On each paper, every article about the murder or trial had been scorched.

"I hope you didn't burn yourself, Dylan."

"No, I managed to grab the papers on the one side that wasn't burning."

"That's good. But do you see what I mean?" Prudy shook her head. "This is exactly what happened last time. It's a warning, don't you think so?"

"A warning or she's trying to tell us something."

"You mean Alex?"

"Yes, maybe she's trying to tell us that everything that's been written about the murder and the trial is inaccurate and we're looking in the wrong places."

"Well, I sure wish she'd find a little less dramatic and dangerous method of telling us. I'm really rather frustrated and a bit concerned. I mean if I hadn't just smelled something burning, that smoldering fire could have become a serious fire. At this point, I'm not sure how to proceed with investigating."

"Do you have any belongings, like clothing, personal items or correspondence that belonged to Alexandra?"

Aunt Maggie interjected excitedly. "There's an old storage trunk up in the attic. I believe there are still some of Alexandra's personal belongings in there. You could take a look. We also have some letters written by the mayor, and if I remember correctly, one or two written by Alexandra. But we've re-read them all several times over the years. There was nothing in the letters that could be of any significance to you regarding the murder mystery."

"Do you think we could go up to the attic now and look through the trunk?"

"You and Prudy can go up there, but I suggest you wait until tomorrow. The single bulb light up there is burned out. You won't be able to see a thing tonight. I meant to change it, but it slipped my mind."

"You shouldn't be climbing up to change that bulb anyway, Aunt Maggie. You could fall and hurt yourself."

"You're probably right, dear. If and when you two go up there, take a new bulb with you and you can change it for me."

"I could come back tomorrow. I'm still working on the article anyway and I have a few more questions. Tomorrow's Friday. What time do you have to be at work, Prudy?"

"Oh, the library isn't open on Fridays during the summer, so I won't be going in. I actually have the whole day off tomorrow and no plans. Why don't you come over tomorrow morning at about eleven."

"It's a date," Dylan said, enthusiastically. Prudy walked Dylan to the door, and just about to leave with his hand on the doorknob, Dylan turned to gaze at Prudy, smiled at her, then kissed her tenderly on the cheek. "Thank your aunt again for a fantastic meal. I'll see you tomorrow. I hope you sleep well. Good night, Prudy."

"Good night, Dylan."

From behind the screen door, Prudy watched Dylan get into his car and slowly drive away. Aunt Maggie walked up behind her niece and put her hand on her shoulder.

"He's a very nice, young man, not to mention intelligent and quite handsome. I like him."

Prudy turned and smiled at her aunt. "Yes, he certainly is nice, intelligent, and definitely handsome. I like him too. He's unlike anyone I've ever met before. He has the manners of someone much older than his actual years, if you know what I mean."

"Yes, I do know what you mean. Perhaps he's an old soul. I think it's great that he's writing an article about the history of Mystic Port, and you are the perfect person to interview for that. I'm excited about it, and for you, dear."

Prudy smiled at her aunt. "Thanks, Aunt Maggie, I'm excited too. It's funny how one day, one person, can change your whole perspective."

"Yes, that's true, dear. And maybe not change just your perspective, but possibly your life."

Well, it's certainly been quite an interesting and eventful day, and I do believe the wine has me feeling quite sleepy. I think I'll head off to bed now."

"I'll be going up soon myself, dear. Good night."

"Good night, Aunt Maggie."

As sleepy as she felt, Prudy did not fall asleep right away. She had so much on her mind. The strange supernatural incident at the museum perplexed her. Maybe the museum really was haunted. She was pretty sure her house was haunted, so she already believed in ghosts and hauntings. It wasn't much of a stretch to think the mansion that housed the museum and library, as old as it was, could be haunted too. But it was Dylan who was foremost on her mind. She liked everything about him. He was smart, handsome, and had a wonderful sense of humor. Prudy found herself anticipating his return the next morning. As the grandfather clock on the landing downstairs chimed eleven times, she finally fell asleep.

At exactly midnight, Prudy stirred and awakened. A gusty summer breeze caused the wind chimes on the front porch to tinkle and her lace curtains to gently billow and sway. She closed her eyes again and listened to the chimes and the rumble of thunder off in the distance.

Soon, the breeze turned into a fierce wind as a nasty storm approached. Leaves rustled in the trees, and what sounded like a faint moaning, sent a shiver down Prudy's spine. She swore she heard her name in the moaning whispers of the wind.

Now, unable to fall back asleep, she got out of bed and decided to make her way to the bathroom. A violent crack of thunder made her jump, and she stubbed her toe on the corner of her vanity.

"Ouch!"

Prudy carefully made her way down the dark hall to the bathroom, the only light being the occasional flash of lightening. Not wanting to injure herself again, she slowly took each step, floorboards creaking beneath her feet, until she finally reached the bathroom. She clicked on the light switch, but the light did not come on. The electricity must have gone out due to the storm. This is not my night, she thought, and then chuckled. Probably another one of Aunt Alex's hauntings.

When she was back in her bedroom, Prudy made her way over to her bed, but stopped dead in her tracks as a spine-shivering chill blanketed her. There was no doubt in her mind there was an unearthly visitor in the room with her. It was the same bone-chilling cold that she'd felt in the library that morning. She quickly got in bed and covered herself with the sheet and blanket, pulling them half up over her head. Finally, due to shear exhaustion, Prudy finally fell asleep again.

Chapter Six

Dylan enthusiastically arrived at the house at 10:50 the following morning.

Good morning, Prudy. I hope you slept well. Was there any more excitement after I left last night?"

"Well, we did have quite a storm blow through here at about midnight last night."

"A real storm this time?"

Prudy laughed. "Yes, a real storm. It was pretty bad, too. The power was off for a good part of the night but luckily came back on early this morning. How about you? Did you sleep well? You certainly look chipper, Dylan."

"Oh, I'm psyched, and I just can't wait to go up to the attic and take a look in that trunk, can you?"

"I have to admit that I'm more than a bit curious, even though I looked through the contents of that trunk many times when I was a kid. I used to spend hours up there. Aunt Maggie would have to coax me to come back downstairs with a promise of freshly baked chocolate chip cookies. But as a young girl, I was more interested in the clothing and jewelry, things I could use to play dress-up, and not clues that might help in solving a century old murder mystery. I am anxious to see if there are any journals or documents, or anything that might help us in our investigation. But as anxious as I am to look around up there, I insist on sitting down for at least ten minutes so I can finish my morning coffee. Care to join me?"

"Sure, I'll have cup."

Prudy smiled and led Dylan back to the kitchen, where Aunt Maggie was sitting, deep in thought with a coffee mug in her hands.

"Good morning Miss, Mrs., oh...forgive me, Aunt Maggie. I'm not sure what would be appropriate for me to call you. Do you have a preference?"

"Well, you can call me Maggie if you'd like. But whatever you'd like to call me would probably be just fine, Dylan. Except for ma'am. Ma'am is definitely out. It makes me feel old," Aunt Maggie said with a giggle."

"Maggie, you're one funny lady. I must say, I haven't met a Beaudicort woman I haven't liked. Beauty, smarts, a sense of humor, and a fantastic cook. What's not to like?"

Aunt Maggie beamed. She enjoyed the company of such a personable and good-looking young man like Dylan. It had been ages since one had visited the house or called on her niece. She truly liked him and felt that he and her niece would make a great couple. But perhaps she was getting a little bit ahead of herself. Only time would tell. But she did have a good feeling about Dylan.

The threesome sat at the oak kitchen table and drank their coffee.

Dylan studied the antique table, running his hand over the top, admiring the grain in the wood.

"I love antiques. This oak table is beautiful. They don't make fine pieces of furniture like this anymore. I know it's quite old, but I can tell it's been very well cared for."

Aunt Maggie smiled. "Thanks Dylan. We love it too. It belonged to Alex, you know."

"Really? You mean this could have been the exact place where that infamous salad was prepared?"

"It could be. But I have serious doubts it was Alexandra who made the salad."

"So, you believe it was Amelia Sanderson, the housekeeper, who prepared the salad, and that she was the murderer?"

"Indeed, I do. I've believed that for many years. She had a bad reputation, you know. She'd had more than one employer who let her go from their employ."

"You don't say. For what reasons I wonder."

"Supposedly, she always worked for high profile and wealthy families, and it was rumored she would have affairs with the man of the house and then blackmail them. If they didn't do what she wanted, she'd threaten to tell their wives about the affair. Blackmail pure and simple."

"You don't think that's what happened with the Beaudicorts, do you?"

"No, I think Samuel deeply loved Alexandra and his life with her and their son. He wouldn't have had an affair. Maybe Amelia tried to seduce the mayor, but he wouldn't comply. She couldn't take the rejection, so she murdered him."

"Geeze, it sounds like she was one unhinged and nasty woman. Do you think she murdered Alexandra too, and why? I mean Alexandra had already been arrested and was in jail. Do you think Amelia probably just hated Alexandra that much?"

"I think she was afraid that Alexandra, with the help of her cousin, was gathering enough evidence to prove that she, Amelia, was the murderer. She also probably hated Alexandra for being the reason her scheme to seduce Samuel had failed. Amelia was obviously psychologically disturbed, probably a sociopath."

"Do you know whatever became of Amelia?"

"No, not really, other than she continued to live in Mystic Port and have a family whose descendants still reside in Mystic Port today. Many of whom believe and continue to say that Alexandra was the murderer. Needless to say, they have nothing to do with us. I try to avoid them as much as possible."

"Wow, that must be difficult for you to have to deal with, especially in a small town like Mystic Port."

"Indeed, and also the reason Prudy and I would like to be able to prove Alexandra's innocence once and for all. Not so much to prove it to them, but more to know we've been right all these years. If there was a way we could prove Alexandra's innocence without implicating Amelia, that would be great, but I'm afraid that's probably impossible."

"I can see your point, I guess. I imagine you presenting proof of Alexandra's innocence by proving Amelia's guilt could ruffle a few feathers in this town."

"Yes, I have no doubt it would."

"What about other townspeople? Do you know how they feel about Alexandra and the murder of her husband?"

"I think the majority of the residents of Mystic Port don't really have an opinion one way or the other. To them, it's ancient history and it doesn't affect them. Most of them don't dislike Prudy or I just because of who we're related to."

"That's good, at least."

All three finished their coffee, and Dylan, who always seemed to be hungry, finished one of Aunt Maggie's delicious cinnamon rolls. Dylan had gulped his coffee, obviously in a hurry to get upstairs to check out the attic and the trunk that had belonged to Alexandra.

Prudy chuckled. "Well, I can see you won't last another minute, Dylan. Before you rip your stitches, let's go up to the attic, shall we?"

"Oh here, Prudy," Maggie said as she handed her niece a light bulb. If one of you could change the bulb up there, I'd appreciate it."

"Of course, Aunt Maggie. I'll let Dylan change it, he's tall."

Prudy led the way upstairs, up to the third floor, then up one small set of steps to the attic. She put her hand on the knob of the door but to her dismay, it wouldn't turn.

"The doorknob won't turn."

"What do you mean? You wouldn't be teasing me would you, Prudy?"

"No, seriously, the knob won't turn, and for as long as I've lived here, I've never known this door to be locked before."

"Here, let me try."

"Be my guest."

Dylan moved up to the last step next to Prudy. She carefully moved aside then down a step, making room for him. He tried the knob, but it wouldn't move at all. "It won't budge. It's locked, I'm sure of it. Do you have a key for this door?"

"Wait, I'll check with Aunt Maggie."

Just then Maggie called from downstairs. "Is everything okay up there?"

"Aunt Maggie, the doorknob won't turn. Could the door possibly be locked?" Prudy yelled down.

"Oh right, I'll be right there, dear. I'll get the key. I forgot that I locked the door last time I was up there." After she had retrieved the key from the desk drawer, Maggie started to make her way up the steps, but as she got to the second flight, an overwhelming, unseen power pulled her back. "I can't move up another step. Something's holding me back," she yelled.

Prudy moved down the steps to get the key from her aunt, thinking her aunt meant that she was tired and was unable to climb up any more steps. Prudy reached out for the key and noticed the look of extreme concern on her aunt's face. "Aunt Maggie, are you okay?"

"I'm okay, but something is holding me back. It feels like I'm glued to this spot. I can't move. Something, or someone, doesn't want us to go into the attic. That's a bad sign. It's a warning. I really don't think you should go up there."

"Dylan, please come down. Aunt Maggie had one of her feelings. We can't go up there today. Something's wrong."

Dylan made his way down the steps, and he and Prudy helped her visibly upset aunt back downstairs and into the living room to sit down on the sofa.

"I know you two must be disappointed. I'm sorry Dylan, but most of these feelings I get are meaningful. But this was not just a feeling. It was like some force was physically holding me back. What I don't understand is, if we're in agreement that Alex is trying to tell us the truth about her husband's demise, then why would she hold us back from finding the evidence we need to exonerate her? That doesn't make sense. Something's not right here. I have a bad feeling, an instinct that we may be in over our heads. I'm worried that we may have an opposing spirit on our hands. I'm going to call Dr. Spelling."

"Who's Dr. Spelling?" Dylan inquired.

Prudy interjected. "He's that poltergeist interventionist I told you about, who we used once before when we were having problems here at the house. He's a bit of a character, quite eccentric, really, but he's the only person in Mystic Port who has any experience at all with this type of situation. I have always wondered though, what he's a doctor of."

Aunt Maggie explained, "Oh, he's not a medical doctor. I believe he has a doctorate degree in a science of some sort. I don't really know how he became an expert in the supernatural."

"What exactly do you think is happening with this poltergeist situation?" Dylan asked.

"I'm thinking there may be two forces, or spirits, we're dealing with here, and they may be opposing each other. I've heard that it's never a good idea to get in the middle of opposing spirits. Things could get downright nasty."

"And possibly even dangerous," added Prudy.

"Prudy dear, please hand me the phone."

Prudy handed the phone to her aunt, who, due to her still superb memory, punched in Dr. Spelling's number by memory. The phone rang five times, and Maggie was just thinking Dr. Spelling might be away, when he answered the phone.

"Hello-o-o-o-o, Dr. Spelling here."

"Hi Doc. This is Maggie Beaudecort."

"Well, I'll be. Maggie Beaudicort, to what do I owe the pleasure? I haven't talked to you since last summer. I hope you're well."

"Yes, I'm fine, doc. But we're having a situation here again at the house. I'm sure you probably remember the problems we were having last summer with our beloved Aunt Alexandra."

"Why yes, of course I do. Are you having problems again?"

"Yes, unfortunately we are. I believe Alexandra is trying to set the record straight about her husband's untimely demise, but that another force, or spirit, is holding her, and us, back from finding the proof we need to be able to do that. We've recently had some what we believe to be supernatural occurrences happen here at the house."

"Hmm...I see. So, you think you may have two unsettled spirits on your hands, do you?"

"Yes, that's exactly what I think. I am of the firm belief that Alexandra did not murder her husband. I'm also strongly of the opinion that Amelia Sanderson was the murderer of both Mayor Beaudicort and Alexandra. If that's the case, then I think it's possible that the spirit of Amelia Sanderson may be the opposing spirit."

"I trust your intuition and judgement, Maggie. If that is indeed the case, the situation you're dealing with can be difficult and even dangerous. I'm glad you called me instead of trying to handle the situation yourself. Let me look at my schedule here. Yes, I happen to be free a bit later this afternoon. I could stop by at about two o'clock. Would that work for you?"

"Oh, yes, and thanks, doc. See you then." Aunt Maggie handed the phone back to Prudy.

"Dr. Spelling will be here at two o'clock. He was glad I contacted him about our situation."

"Yes, I think it was wise of you to contact Dr. Spelling, Aunt Maggie. I do hope he's able to help us out. If it's true that there are two unsettled spirits opposing each other in this house, it's not something we should probably try to handle ourselves."

"That's exactly what he said." Maggie looked at her watch. "Well...it's only 12:30, and since we have some time on our hands, how about we have some lunch? I have a lovely chicken salad made. It's in the refrigerator."

Dylan smiled. "My mom used to make chicken salad. Sounds great and I'm ravenous."

"Dylan, I do believe you must have a hollow leg."

He looked at Maggie and laughed. "I've never heard that expression before. But I do get it. It is rather funny, and I have always had a hearty appetite."

The threesome again sat around the antique oak table and enjoyed chicken salad sandwiches, pickles and some chips and freshly brewed iced tea.

"This chicken salad is delicious. Almost as good as my mom's," Dylan said with a wink. "And the iced tea is really good.

Maggie smiled. "I'm glad you like the chicken salad and the iced tea, Dylan. I'll let you in on a little secret about the iced tea. Instead of putting sugar or another sweetener in it, I put a little bit of orange juice in it."

"Well, it's very good."

Everyone was hungry so there was no further discussion of ghosts or a possible poltergeist until after they'd finished eating.

Dylan's inquisitiveness got the better of him. The thought of there actually being a poltergeist in the house filled him with both angst and delight. And then there was the situation with Prudy. He really liked her a lot. Although they had only met a day ago, so much had happened in that time. He was aware that she seemed to truly like him as well. He had hoped he'd meet someone special. But never had he expected to meet someone as beautiful and intelligent as Prudy. She matched wit with him every step of the way and enjoyed a lot of the same things he did: sports, history, art, music, to name a few. And their collaboration with the article Dylan was writing, as well as with their investigation and search for the truth about the murder of the mayor made them quite the team.

"A penny for your thoughts," Aunt Maggie interrupted his daydreaming.

"Yeah, Dylan. Like Earth to Dylan. Do you copy?" Prudy teased.

"Oh...yes, sorry to have spaced out like that. I'm just trying to wrap my head around everything that's happened in the last two days. It's been quite an adventure so far."

"Don't spend too much time trying to wrap your head around it. You'll give yourself a headache." Maggie teased.

Prudy asked her aunt and Dylan what they thought they'd like to do while waiting the hour or so before Dr. Spelling was due to arrive.

"I guess it wouldn't be such a good idea to start playing Texas Hold-um, would it?" Aunt Maggie asked in jest.

"No, poker's not for me, I'm afraid. I'm not very good at it and I'm also a bit of a sore loser," Dylan replied.

"I know what we can do. Would you like to see the old photos of Alex?" Prudy asked excitedly.

"You bet I would!" Dylan said eagerly.

Prudy went to the pantry room and opened the bottom drawer of a very large built in cabinet. She pulled out an old hatbox that was full of pictures. Most of them were from her childhood and of her parents, Christmases long ago, and several pictures of the house. But there were two very old photos in the hatbox of her lovely Great Aunt Alexandra. In one of the photos Alexandra was posed on a chaise lounge and she was holding an ostrich feather fan in front of her mouth. In the second photograph she was standing in front of a fireplace. In both photos Alexandra was wearing a light-colored lacy blouse with a high neckline and puffy-shouldered sleeves and a dark-colored skirt. The photos appeared to have been taken there in the house.

Dylan held the photos and looked at them closely. "These photos are amazing, and Alexandra is beautiful, even in everyday clothing. She has a faint almost mischievous smile, rather looking like the cat who swallowed the canary."

"Let me see the one you're looking at, Dylan," Prudy said, studying the picture closer. "I see what you mean. I wonder who or what she was thinking about when this picture was taken.

"I hope she wasn't planning a murder." Dylan said wryly."

"Ha! I really don't think my Aunt Alex was capable of murder."

"Yes, I know. I was joking. I don't either. Just look at her. She looks as innocent as can be, obviously happy and content. That's not the look of a murderer. One thing is for sure; she was an extremely beautiful woman."

"So, you've said about a dozen times since we met," Prudy said, with a slight note of sarcasm in her voice.

"And I've also made the point of saying that I thought all of the Beaudicort women are beautiful."

"Yes, that's true." Prudy smiled.

"Do you have any pictures in the box of her husband, Mayor Beaudicort?"

Aunt Maggie chimed in. "You know, I don't think there are any photos of the mayor in this box, but I do think I have a picture of him that was cut out of the newspaper a few years ago. I'm not even sure Prudy has seen the picture."

Maggie excused herself and went into the dining room and opened one of the drawers of an old antique mahogany hutch that held antique fine china and several beautiful antique crystal vases. Inside the drawer was a folder filled with newspaper articles about the house and the local history of Mystic Port and the Beaudicort family. She took the entire folder into the kitchen and sat back down at the oak table. She leafed through the articles until she found the one she was looking for, pulled it out of the folder and looked at the picture that accompanied the article.

A look of total bewilderment came across her face as she closely examined the picture. "Oh my, I don't believe this." she said, not even realizing she was speaking out loud.

"What is it, Aunt Maggie? Are you okay? You look like you've seen a ghost."

Speechless, she said nothing but simply handed the cut out piece of newspaper to her niece. Prudy took one look at the picture of her great uncle, the mayor, and sank back in her chair. She felt her heart beating faster and a flush came to her cheeks. "I don't believe this. How is this possible?"

"What is it?" Dylan pleaded, and unable to hold back another second, took the clipping from Prudy. "I don't believe it," he said as he slowly sat back down at the table and just starred at the photograph of Mayor Samuel Beaudicort. "This is unbelievable."

The three of them sat there looking at each other for a good minute or so but said nothing. The silence became unnerving as each of them was trying to make sense of the rather strange occurrences that continued to accompany their investigation of Samuel Beaudicort's murder and what this latest development could possibly mean, if anything.

Dylan shook his head, finding it impossible to make sense of things. Prudy seemed to be in a state of shock. She got up from the table and started pacing the room. Then she stared out the kitchen window looking out at the beautiful gardens, just pondering everything. After a moment, she sat back down at the table but said nothing.

Chapter Seven

The three of them continued to sit in silence for several minutes, each trying to make some kind of sense out of the strange things that had occurred during the last two days.

Aunt Maggie finally broke the silence. "Does anyone else think it's got to be more than a coincidence that you, Dylan, are the spitting image of Samuel Beaudicort?"

"I...yes, it's definitely got to be more than a coincidence. I'm totally dumbfounded, actually."

"Dylan, is there any chance you're related to him, and us?"

Prudy, who up to this point had remained silent, finally spoke up. "I really hope that's not the case."

Of course she didn't want to be related to Dylan. She was developing feelings for him. What if, by some chance, it turned out that Dylan was related to Samuel Beaudicort, and her? What if he ended up believing that Alexandra actually did murder her husband? How would he feel about her then? Would he hate her?

"No, there is no way I'm related to your family. My family and our descendants are from down on the East Coast, near Philadelphia. We're descended from a pretty small clan of Irish immigrants, the McClintocks. I don't know one relative that's any part French."

Prudy sighed in relief. "But Monroe's not an Irish name, is it?"

"Well yes, actually it can be either Irish or Scottish. In this case, a McClintock married a Scottish born immigrant named Monroe back in the late 1800's. From what I understand, it caused quite the family scandal back then."

Maggie laughed. "You don't say. It's nice to know we're not the only family with a scandal in their history." Aunt Maggie was fascinated with family histories and genealogy. "How do you know so much about your family history, Dylan?"

"My father's an English literature professor at the University of Pennsylvania and his hobby is family genealogy. I can assure you that if the name Beaudicort or any French ancestor had shown up in his research, I'd know about it."

"Now that is interesting," Maggie said with a grin. "Genealogy has always fascinated me. Did you know that Princess Diana was related to George Washington?"

"No, I didn't know that, but I'm sure my father does. He knows the genealogy of a lot of famous and historical figures."

Prudy looked closely at the newspaper photo of her Great Uncle Samuel Beaudicort again. "Well, you know, they say there are only something like thirty different basic facial appearances in the world, and that everyone has at least one double of themselves running around somewhere. I guess that could be the case here."

Dylan eased his way over to stand next to Prudy. "I can see you're upset about this, but I'm sure we're not related. If Mayor Beaudicort were a relative of mine, my father would have told me. As I mentioned, his hobby is our ancestry, and he has included me in his research. I've seen our ancestry chart, and no one by the name of Beaudicort is listed on the chart."

Prudy smiled at him, relieved. "Yes, I'm sure you're right. But it is kind of freaky how much you look like him."

"You're telling me."

"I certainly can say I know the feeling."

"Yes, I guess you do."

Aunt Maggie was actually relieved too as she truly loved her niece and had been silently hoping she'd find a nice, young man to become involved with, and she'd already been hoping Dylan might be that man. "So, Dylan, if your family's from the Philadelphia area, how did you end up here in New England?"

"I went to The University of Rhode Island majoring in journalism."

"I hear they have an excellent journalism curriculum there. But what made you stay in this area after graduation?"

"You know, I had a tough time deciding to stay here, mostly because of being so far away from my family. But I found a job in Newport right after I graduated. It wasn't a job in journalism, but it kept me going until I could find a permanent job as a journalist."

"What job did you have?" Prudy asked

Dylan smiled as he talked about the job he had in Newport, on the crew of an old, restored frigate, as they sailed sightseers around Narragansett Bay. "I really like living in this area. It's certainly beautiful, and to live near the ocean, that's a definite plus. Besides, journalists come a dime a dozen in New York and Philly, and I was afraid I wouldn't find a job back home. One day I saw an ad online that the Coastal Press needed a journalist, so I applied for the job and here I am."

"Well, I'm very glad you did."

Just then the doorbell rang. Aunt Maggie glanced at her watch. "Well now, that must be Dr. Spelling. It's straight up two o'clock."

The three of them went into the living room, curious and anxious to hear what Dr. Spelling would have to say about the whole poltergeist situation and the possibility of opposing spirits inhabiting the family home. Aunt Maggie opened the front door and welcomed the good doctor. Dr. Spelling, who was a rather short and stout man, walked warily into the house, trying to get a sense of any supernatural energy that inhabited it as he passed through the front door into the living room.

"Dr. Spelling, I'd like to introduce you to Mr. Monroe, a journalist with the Coastal Press, who's here to do an interview for the town's 250th anniversary."

Doctor Spelling shook hands with Dylan. "It's a pleasure to meet you, Mr. Monroe."

"Please, call me Dylan."

"Very well then, Dylan." Looking through heavy, black-rimmed eyeglasses, the doctor turned his attention back to Maggie.

"And you remember my niece, Prudy. Dylan is interviewing her for the article he's writing."

"Yes, of course. It's always a pleasure to see you, Prudy. You know you're lucky, Dylan. There's no better person to interview than the town's historian for an article about Mystic Port and its rather colorful history," he said with a raise of his eyebrows. "She's quite knowledgeable, as I'm sure you're aware."

Dylan smiled, "Yes, she certainly knows quite a lot about the history of Mystic Port and its former occupants."

"Indeed. Now, about your dueling spirits, how about we all sit down and discuss the recent events that caused you to contact me again."

"Of course, but let's go into the kitchen and I'll put on a pot of coffee."

The group went into the kitchen and sat around the antique oak table. Dr. Spelling touched the table, then waived both hands back and forth over it. "I believe I'm getting a supernatural vibration coming from this table. Is this the original table owned by the Beaudicort family?"

"Yes, it is, and it might have significance to both Alexandra and Amelia Sanderson," Maggie said.

"Interesting," Dr. Spelling said as he scratched his chin.

Once the coffee was served, Aunt Maggie explained the recent events that led her to believe that the spirit causing the poltergeist, which she had previously suspected was no longer in the house, had either returned or never left.

"But now I'm worried that there are two separate spirits, or ghosts, if you will."

"What makes you think that, Maggie?" Dr. Spelling inquired as he removed his glasses and cleaned the lenses with a handkerchief he took from his suit coat pocket.

"It's a strong feeling I have. I believe the one spirit must be Alexandra. It seems that almost every time we discuss anything regarding the mayor's murder, her spirit leaves us some type of evidence, or she makes some kind of statement trying to tell us she's innocent. But then there also seems to be an opposing energy or spirit who is trying to keep us from finding the evidence or is destroying that evidence."

"Can you give me an example?"

"Of course. Dylan and Prudy were going up to the attic to find some of Alexandra's belongings that are in an old trunk up there. They were hoping to perhaps find something that would help in proving her innocence, like maybe a diary or journal or something. But when they got up there, the doorknob on the attic door would not turn. I'd forgotten I had locked the door the last time I was up there. Anyway, I was down at the bottom of the steps to the third floor and had the attic door key in my hand. I tried to go up the steps to give Prudy the key, but I couldn't move. It felt like I was glued to the spot where I was standing. An unseen force was holding me back. And I had the definite feeling that the force, or spirit, meant business."

"I see," said Dr. Spelling, looking a bit troubled and shaking his head. "You know, I've dealt with a few similar situations in the past, several years ago. But I never heard of a spirit who was able to physically hold someone back from doing something. That must have been frightening. And it's not my intention to scare you, but sometimes things can get out of control in such situations. So, I have to ask you seriously, other than curiosity, is there a reason why you feel you have to dig this up again and investigate?"

"I can answer that," Maggie said quickly. "Prudy and I are the direct descendants of Alexandra and Samuel Beaudicort. Prudy even looks like Alexandra. And although we never met her, we both feel a real connection with her. To us, she's family. I guess you could say we love her. And we don't believe she was capable of murder. With this town's big anniversary coming up, we'd like to set the record straight on behalf of Alexandra. There are many people in this town who only know part of the story or some of the history, and they believe Alexandra to be a murderous witch. God rest her soul. I'd like to be able to prove her innocence. If I'd been unjustly accused of a crime I didn't commit, especially murder, and then died, I'd hope someone would care enough to try to prove my innocence."

"I see. So, it is rather important to you."

"Yes, but let me also say that I don't want to put anyone, especially my niece or Dylan in harm's way."

Dr. Spelling pushed his glasses back up on his nose and looked seriously at Maggie. "This is quite the conundrum, isn't it? But I have to say that I, nor anybody else can give you any guarantee that someone might not get hurt if you insist on going ahead with investigating this. When you're dealing with an angry poltergeist, bad things can happen."

Maggie looked quite unhappy. "But even when we're just talking about Alexandra, it seems the bad spirit acts up now. And we can't do things like go up to the attic? I mean, isn't there a way to get rid of an unwelcome spirit?"

"Well, it's been done, usually by a team of highly skilled psychic mediums who also have a priest with them who is experienced in exorcism, in the event that the spirit is evil. But trying to find someone who's experienced with this sort of thing would be difficult. And if you did find them, I can't imagine how expensive it would be to hire them. And I'm sure there would be no guarantee that the hauntings would stop. Even if the hauntings stopped for a while, there's no assurance that things wouldn't start up again at some point later."

Prudy appeared quite concerned. "Dr. Spelling, you said bad things can happen when dealing with an angry poltergeist. What kind of bad things are we talking about?"

"If a spirit is angry enough and determined, there's the potential for fires, serious accidents, and worse."

"Do you have any firsthand knowledge of a poltergeist gone bad?"

"Unfortunately, yes, I do. About thirty years ago, A friend of my brother's was found dead at the bottom of the basement steps in his house. There wasn't a mark on him, but the authorities said he had suffered a broken neck that must have happened when he fell down the steps. He either tripped and fell, or possibly, he was pushed. He had been investigating a murder that happened in that house in the basement back in the 1950's. Several months after his death, his son was cleaning out his office in the basement and came across a folder that had been partially burned, but contained the remnants of some old police reports that actually pointed the finger of guilt at the son's grandmother, who they think killed their housekeeper in a fit of jealous rage. As it was rumored, his grandfather had been having an affair with the housekeeper, and his wife found out, took matters into her own hands and murdered her. But they didn't have enough evidence to convict. A week later, the son was back down in the basement doing some more investigating about his grandmother having been taken in for questioning regarding the death of the housekeeper, and a fire broke out on the main floor above him."

Prudy couldn't contain herself. "What happened to the son? Did he die in the fire?"

"No, by the grace of God he didn't die. But he was badly burned and was in the hospital for several months. The firemen pulled him out just before the house became a roaring inferno and then collapsed completely into a rubble of black wood and ashes."

"Good Lord," Aunt Maggie said, and covered her mouth.

Prudy asked, "Do you happen to know the name of the housekeeper who was murdered?"

"No, I'm afraid I don't know the name of the housekeeper. I know what you're probably wondering, but this poltergeist situation was in Vermont. I highly doubt the housekeeper was related to the Sanderson family here in Mystic Port."

"I'm sure you're probably right. So do you have any recommendations as to what we should do, Dr. Spelling?"

"When you are investigating on their turf, and especially if there are two opposing forces, my expert advice is you shouldn't conduct the investigation there in that place where they are residing. So, you see, I strongly suggest you give up your investigation, at least here at the house. Did all these mishaps only happen here at the house?"

Dylan and Prudy shot sideways glances at each other. Prudy then told Dr. Spelling about what had happened at the museum.

"Hmm... That's quite interesting and unusual. Hauntings by the same spirit or spirits usually only occur in the one place, basically where they reside. Perhaps there's a connection between both spirits and the museum. This is the first time I've ever heard of the possibility of a spirit being able to transport to another location, if that's indeed the case. Was there any damage or was anyone hurt?"

"No, not really, except for a pencil hitting me in the forehead. I wasn't scared and whatever it was, I didn't feel like it was angry or meant to cause any real harm. It felt more like whatever it was, they were trying to get our attention."

"That's good, I'm glad there was no serious damage and that you weren't seriously hurt."

Dr. Spelling got up to leave, and before walking out the door he turned, and with a most serious expression on his face he said, "Please heed my warning. I'd hate to see anything untoward happen to any of you. An unsettled poltergeist can be quite dangerous. Good afternoon."

Chapter Eight

"He wasn't really of much help, was he? Aunt Maggie asked dejectedly. "I thought he might come up with some plan or at least suggest something we could do. Instead, all we got was a warning."

Prudy looked at Dylan, who seemed disappointed, and then at her aunt, who was obviously quite upset at the prospect of having an angry, unsettled spirit inhabiting her home. But Prudy noticed something else about her dear aunt. She looked a bit tired and drained. Maybe all this talk about spirits and poltergeists was taking a toll on her aging aunt. She was genuinely concerned about her aunt's wellbeing and would have to seriously consider what Dr. Spelling had advised.

Prudy forced a smile and said, "Well, how about we call it a day. I'm beat, and there's nothing we're going to decide or accomplish any more today."

Dylan seemed to pick up on Prudy's concern for her aunt. "I agree. I'm quite wiped out myself. I think I'll say good afternoon to you lovely ladies. Prudy, we do need to finish the interview, so I'll give you a call soon."

"Yes, of course, the interview. I'll wait to hear from you, Dylan."

"Aunt Maggie, thank you for a wonderful lunch," Dylan said as he extended his hand to her.

"It was my pleasure, Dylan. You are welcome here any time."

After Dylan left and dinner time was approaching, Prudy decided she'd take care of preparing a light dinner for herself and her aunt. She made a pot of decaffeinated tea and she and Maggie sat in the kitchen at the antique oak table talking as they nibbled on some leftovers.

"So dear, what do you think about this poltergeist situation and your investigation in trying to prove Alex's innocence?"

"I'm thinking it would be wise to take Dr. Spelling's advice. I'd like to continue investigating, but not here at the house."

"Oh good, that's what I was hoping you'd say. I'm not thrilled with the idea of there possibly being an angry spirit here in this house. And opposing spirits, if that's the case, I'm definitely not happy with that prospect. But to be honest with you, I really don't think anything we do, or don't do, will make that much of a difference. Of course, I think we should be careful not to aggravate the situation. I don't think we should do things like go to the attic, at least for now. It's obvious the angry spirit does not want us up there."

"What are the chances we'd find anything in Alex's old trunk that would have anything to do with the murder anyway? If I remember correctly from when I was a kid, that trunk in the attic only contains some old clothing and purses that we've already gone through, and some more old photos. There was no correspondence, no journals, or books that I remember."

"No, me either. Nothing of any pertinence, anyway. I don't think we should discuss the truth or innocence of either party here in the house. But I'm wondering, dear, just how will you investigate? You've already been through all the books and newspaper articles written on the case, haven't you?"

"Yes, at the library. But that was some time ago and there was a lot of information. Maybe I missed something." Prudy leaned forward a bit in her chair. "You know, I was thinking that I'd visit Gertrude at her antique shop tomorrow. She's got tuns of old books and memorabilia from Mayor Beaudicort's election and his unfortunate demise. She may be able to help me out."

"Yes, I'm sure she'd love to help you in whatever way she can, and she's very fond of you, dear. Remember, Gerty and your mom were very close growing up. They were practically inseparable. She's also been a dear friend to me all these years. Oh, and I just remembered that she has the gown Alex wore in those paintings in the museum. I believe she also has some other clothing that belonged to Alex. I'd say it's definitely worth a visit to her."

Maggie smiled at her niece, appreciating her spunk, but also about her being smart in proceeding with her investigation but with caution. Maggie finished her cup of tea and rubbed her eyes.

"I know it's early, but I think I'm going to go to bed. This has been one heck of a long day!"

"Yes, it certainly has been."

Maggie rose and hugged her niece. "Good night, dear."

"Good night, Auntie. I hope you sleep well."

"You too, dear."

After Maggie had gone upstairs, Prudy continued to sit at the table and ponder the entire situation. She trusted Dr. Spelling and his instincts, but she had no intention of giving up on the investigation entirely. She would definitely continue to investigate, but not here at the house, mostly out of concern for her aunt. She didn't want to anger an unsettled spirit that obviously still resided here.

Prudy tossed and turned in bed that night, sleep eluding her. But it wasn't the investigation or thoughts about the poltergeist or the article that kept her awake. She was thinking about Dylan and how much she liked him and how attracted she was to him. After all, what was not to like? She couldn't think of a thing. If she'd tried to imagine the ideal man for her, it would be him.

He was unlike any other man she'd ever met. Dare she think that he was sent to her, that it was fate that he was assigned to come here to Mystic Port to interview her? She didn't even know if she believed in fate. She'd never had to consider it before.

Chapter Nine

Prudy awoke early the next morning and was glad it was Saturday so she would have some free time to focus on the next step in her investigation. She was anxious to call Gertrude to see if it would be alright with her if she stopped by her antique shop to have a look through Alex's things. But she'd have to wait another hour or so to call her. As with most of the shops and boutiques in town, Gertrude's shop didn't open until ten o'clock on a Saturday.

Prudy was just finishing up a cup of coffee when her cell phone rang. She was delighted to see the call was from Dylan.

"Hello, Dylan."

"Good morning, Prudy. I trust you slept well."

"Yes, okay, and you?"

"Like a baby. So, what are you up to today? Are you available to discuss the article?"

"I'm thinking of going into town to visit a friend of Aunt Maggie's and mine. She's a woman by the name of Gertrude who has an antique shop. She has some memorabilia from Mayor Beaudicort's campaign and election, as well as some of Alexandra's belongings, including that beautiful gown she was wearing in the portrait you were so taken with."

"Are you serious? I'd love to see that gown. At the risk of sounding too pushy, would you mind if I tagged along with you?"

"No, not at all. I was going to ask you if you wanted to come with me anyway. Can you meet in front of the library at about 9:45?"

"Yes, that will be fine. I'll be there. See you then."

Prudy smiled, pleased that Dylan had called her, and also pleased that he'd be accompanying her to visit Gertrude at her shop.

When Prudy arrived at the library almost ten minutes early, Dylan was already parked out in front waiting for her.

"Gosh, Dylan. Are you a bit over-anxious or what?" Prudy joked.

Dylan chuckled. "Yes, I admit it. There's something about your Aunt Alexandra, well, I just can't get her, or you, for that matter, out of my mind."

Prudy smiled shyly and blushed. "Well, we're almost twenty minutes early and it only takes two minutes to get to Gertrude's shop from here. How about we stop at the Brew Awhile and get some coffee?"

"Great idea, hop in. I'll drive."

"Okay." Prudy quickly got in the passenger seat next to Dylan. He started the ignition and put the car in gear. Before he drove off, he turned and smiled at Prudy. "You look beautiful, Prudy."

"Oh, thanks." Prudy smiled.

Dylan, remembering the route they had driven the previous day, drove to the town center of Mystic Port and parked in front of the Brew Awhile Café. As they approached the entrance, they stopped to look at the special of the day.

Dylan joked, "I'm bummed. No more Frothy Frog, and Lethargic Leopard doesn't sound like it would be a very good pick-me-up."

Prudy laughed. "Looks like it will have to be basic black again today."

They got their coffees to go. On their way out of the coffee house, Dylan noticed a few tables and chairs in a small garden area where, if you chose to, you could sit and enjoy your coffee and the scenery.

Hey, Prudy, let's have our coffee out here instead of drinking it on the run. We have time, don't we?"

Prudy looked at her watch. It was now only 9:45 a.m., and Gertrude's didn't open until 10:00 a.m.

"Sure, we have a few minutes to spare, and there's really no rush. It's not like we have an appointment with Gertrude, although I know you're anxious about seeing Alex's things, especially the gold, satin gown she's wearing in the portrait you were so taken with."

The two of them sat down at a small table near the cherub fountain in the back corner of the garden. It was a fair, late summer morning with a slight breeze and just a few billowy, white clouds in the sky.

"Ah yes, that stunning gold gown from the portrait. It will be interesting to see the actual gown that she wore. I just hope no angry spirit follows us to Gertrude's."

"Oh, I really don't think we need to worry about that. Actually, I don't remember any time when I had an incident with the angry spirit, and it wasn't at the house."

"Have you already forgotten about the other day in the museum? Don't you now think that was a spirit causing such a commotion?"

Prudy tilted her head as she contemplated this question. "A spirit, possibly, but not an angry spirit, I don't think so. It could have been Alex just trying to get our attention."

"Prudy, you told me you think you've been in the presence of both spirits, Alexandra and whoever or whatever the angry spirit is, right? Is there a distinct difference between the two?"

"Oh yes, no question about it, most definitely."

"So, what do you think about the spirit in the museum yesterday? Was it good or bad?"

"Well, remember, you were the one in the room with it. I was still in the library when you saw whatever it was. Did you get a feeling for whether it was a good or evil entity?"

"I can't say I felt threatened or afraid, except for the objects flying through the air. That could have been a lot worse. Like a pencil in my eye or something."

"One thing I've noticed is that the angry, or evil, spirit makes me feel extremely cold. And I don't mean just feeling that pocket of cold air that I felt in the library yesterday. It's a cold that feels like it goes through your entire body and lingers."

"But didn't you say you were cold yesterday? You were wrapping your hands around your coffee cup trying to warm up."

"I was just a bit chilled. It didn't last long."

"Then I think I'd have to say the spirit in the museum yesterday was good and was just trying to get our attention for some reason."

Prudy nodded in agreement, then glanced at her watch.

"Time to go?"

"Yes, I guess we can go now. I can tell you're chomping at the bit," Prudy said, teasingly.

The couple arrived at Gertrude's Visions of the Past Antiques Shop, which was actually in a grand, old Victorian house, at two minutes after ten, surprising Gertrude as they followed her in the door. She had just arrived herself and had been out front sweeping some leaves and dirt off the sidewalk.

"Prudy, dear, how are you? You look lovely as always. It's so good to see you. I haven't seen you since your Aunt Maggie's birthday." Gertrude smiled at Dylan. "And who might this handsome, young man be?"

Dylan extended his hand to Gertrude. "Hi, I'm Dylan Monroe from the Coastal Press. I'm writing an article about Prudy, the museum, and the history of the town for the 250th celebration next month. I've accompanied her here in hopes of seeing some of the Beaudicort memorabilia."

Prudy chimed in. "Mr. Monroe is particularly interested in seeing the gold gown Alexandra was wearing in the large portrait of her that's hanging in the museum."

"Oh, the gown. Why yes, of course you can see it. Maybe Prudy can even model it for you. Are you a decent photographer, Mr. Monroe?"

"Ah...no, unfortunately that's not one of my talents."

"Well, my nephew, Ernest, is a professional photographer, and a pretty good one at that. I can give him a call and ask him to come over if you'd like."

Dylan smiled. "If it wouldn't be too much trouble, that would be fantastic. I think it's a great idea, don't you, Prudy?"

Prudy looked a bit hesitant. "What, you mean you want to take pictures of me wearing the gown? I'd have to take a look at the dress first to see if I think it would even fit me."

Gertrude eyed Prudy up and down. You look so much like Alexandra. It wouldn't surprise me a bit if the gown fit you perfectly. Come to the back and we'll take a look at it and see what you think."

Dylan and Prudy followed Gertrude to the back of the shop. Gertrude opened a wardrobe bag that hung among others on a wardrobe carrier. She gently pulled out the elegant, satin gown. Prudy had seen the gown many years previously but had forgotten just how absolutely stunning it was.

"It's truly gorgeous, isn't it?"

"Yes, it is, Prudy. And I do think it looks like it would fit you. What do you think, Mr. Monroe?"

"I think I'd very much like Prudy to try it on. And if it fits, then maybe you could call that photographer nephew of yours to take some photos."

Prudy was still unsure if she liked the idea of having pictures taken. "Well, let's see first if the gown fits. If it does fit and Ernie is going to take pictures, I'd like to style my hair and maybe put on some makeup. I'll have to run home to grab a few things."

"Prudy dear, there will be no need for you to run home. I have everything you'll need here in the dressing room," Gertrude assured her.

Chapter Ten

Gertrude escorted Prudy to the dressing room where she could change into the gown. There was a full length mirror in the room, although it was nothing more than what had been a utility room years earlier, the space was now set up to be a dressing room with a vanity and all sorts of vintage accessories.

Prudy took off her jeans and blouse and put them on an antique lady's chair that was next to the vanity. She couldn't step into the gown, but had to have Gertrude hoist it over her head and pull it down into place. Once the dress was on and had been straightened out, Prudy turned around to look in the mirror as Gertrude gasped in awe.

Prudy eyed herself in the mirror. The gown fit her like it was made just for her.

"My goodness, Prudy. You look stunning and so much like your Aunt Alexandra. How about sitting down at the vanity and I'll put your hair up the way she had hers in the portrait."

"Okay, thank you." Prudy sat down as Gertrude stood behind her and fiddled with her beautiful, long, dark hair.

"Let me look in this drawer and see if I still have one of those hair rats to use under your hair to give it that full puffed out effect."

Prudy crinkled her nose and gave Gertrude a funny look in the mirror. "What's a hair rat?"

"I know, it sounds weird, but that's what they called the accessory the Victorian and Edwardian women used to add height and girth to their hair. It's really just a mound of hair, like a bun, and it's used under the hair. But I can't seem to find it, and as thick as your hair is, I'm thinking we probably don't need to use it. You know, I think I have an antique hair comb in the front of the shop in one of the display cases. I'll go get it. I'll be right back."

As Gertrude went into the main room, Dylan looked up from a vintage magazine he was reading.

"Does the gown fit Prudy?"

"Oh yes it does, it fits her perfectly, almost as if it was made for her. I'm doing up her hair, so she looks like Alexandra did in the portrait. Then I'll send her out to model it for you. I think you'll like what you see. Then I'll call Ernest so he can come and take some photos. This is so exciting!"

Dylan smiled, both at Gertrude's obvious enthusiasm, and at the thought of how beautiful Prudy must look in that gown. He couldn't wait to see her.

Gertrude found the beautiful antique hair comb she wanted to use and took it back to the dressing room. After she had finished styling Prudy's hair, Gertrude stood back and looked approvingly at her.

"Here, all you need is a touch of blush and some mascara, and...oh, in the portrait Alexandra was holding a fan in front of her, obscuring her mouth. I think I have one of those up front in a drawer. Wait until your Mr. Monroe sees you!"

Prudy stood up and looked in the full-length mirror that hung on the back of the door. She herself was astonished at how much she really did look like her Aunt Alexandra did in the large portrait in the museum.

"Let's go show you off to Dylan!"

Gertrude led the way with Prudy close behind, to the front of the shop where Dylan was eagerly waiting to see how she looked in the gown. As she entered the room he slowly turned to look at her, stunned to see the amazing beauty standing before him as she modeled the exquisite gown. As much as he had anticipated how beautiful Prudy would look, she surpassed his expectations. His mouth dropped open and he found himself speechless for a good twenty seconds. It was like Alexandra Beaudicort had come back to life and was standing right in front of him.

"Well, do you approve?" Prudy beseeched him, as she slowly turned around modeling for him.

"I do believe your Mr. Monroe is at a loss for words, dear."

"Prudy, you look beautiful...stunning actually, and from what I can remember, exactly like Alexandra did in the portrait. I wish we had a picture of the portrait so we could compare and use it as a model to stage you for the photograph."

Gertrude tapped the side of her face, smiled. "You know, I do have a picture of the portrait, a cutout from an article that was in the newspaper a few years ago. Let me take a look in the office and see if I can find it. Oh, and to call Ernest. I'll be right back," Gertrude said, with exuberant excitement in her voice.

She returned a few moments later and excitedly held out the newspaper clipping with the picture of the portrait.

"Here it is! Wait until you see it and how much Prudy resembles Alexandra in the portrait. She's a dead ringer for her!"

Dylan took the newspaper clipping and sat down in an old, antique armchair, looking first at the article picture, then at Prudy. He did this several times, a smile toying with his lips.

"Well, let me see it, Dylan, and what do you think?"

Dylan handed the clipping to her. "What I think is, all we need is a white Victorian fan for Prudy to hold, and we can recreate the portrait picture."

Gertrude was rummaging through some drawers in an old bureau and pulled out an antique, white fan from a plastic bag and presented it to Dylan.

"Now, if you two will follow me into the study, I think you'll be very happy to see the French bench I have in there that may have actually been the one Alexandra was posed on when the portrait was painted. It certainly looks exactly the same as the one Alexandra was sitting on in the other painting hanging next to her portrait in the museum. Most of the furniture in there was from the mayor's office, so it could be the exact bench that was used. Ernest is on his way." Gertrude beamed with delight. "This is so exciting!"

Chapter Eleven

Dylan looked at the bench and then at the picture of the portrait. It looked to be the same exact style, and he agreed that it very well could be the one Alexandra was sitting on when she posed for the portrait.

Gertrude could not contain herself. "So, what do you think?"

"I think it will work perfectly."

Prudy smiled at Dylan as she thought about what a thoughtful man he was. Gertrude smiled at him also, appreciating his kind thoughtfulness.

Just then a friendly male voice could be heard from the front room. "Hello, where are you, Aunt Gertrude?"

"Oh, that would be my nephew, Ernest. We're out here in the study, Ernie."

Ernest, who was an auburn-haired young man with piercing green eyes, entered the room with a broad smile. Prudy introduced the friendly, young man to Dylan. The two men shook hands. But Ernie couldn't take his eyes off Prudy.

"So, I'm guessing you want me to photograph Prudy?"

Gertrude explained their plan to her nephew with great enthusiasm.

"So, what do you think, Ernie?"

"I think it's a fantastic idea. Prudy, you look so much like your Aunt Alexandra does in the portrait hanging in the museum. Quite beautiful, actually."

Prudy smiled shyly. "Thanks, Ernie. Do you think we can recreate the portrait?"

"I don't see why not. Dylan, can you pull the bench out to sit in front of the wall over there, across from the window so we can catch the natural light from outside?"

Dylan moved the bench and motioned for Prudy to sit down and hold the fan in front of her mouth, just as Alexandra had been positioned in the portrait. Prudy did so. Ernie called out instructions as he looked at the photo of the portrait.

"Prudy, turn your face a bit more to your right. Good, now you should hold the fan in your right hand and cover just up to the top of your upper lip. That's perfect! Now, smile because it affects how the rest of your face looks, especially your eyes. Great. Now, tilt your head ever so slightly to the right, keep smiling and lower your gaze. Perfect!"

Ernie clicked picture after picture while standing at slightly different places and at various angles, until he was satisfied that they'd get a great photo.

"Prudy, you're a natural model. I think we're finished. I'm sure we'll get a good photo."

Prudy set down the fan and smiled. "That was quick. When do you think you'll have the photos ready, Ernie?"

"I'm going to go straight home and develop them right away. I can call you when I'm finished and you can pick them up if you'd like. Or, I can give them to Aunt Gertrude, whichever you'd prefer."

Gertrude said quite quickly, "Oh, please bring them over here, Ernie. I can't wait to see them. Prudy, I'll call you as soon as Ernie delivers them, if that's okay."

"Great, that will be fine. Ernie, what do I owe you for taking the photos?"

"For you, Prudy, nothing. You can owe me a coffee or something."

"Well, that's a great deal. Thanks, Ernie."

"Of course, my pleasure."

Dylan walked across the room to speak to Ernie. "Listen, Ernie. You know I'm writing an article about Mystic Port, Prudy, and her connection to Alexandra, in the Coastal Press for the 250th anniversary next month. Would you be willing to allow us to use the photograph in the article?"

"Sure, as long as you mention that I was the photographer. I could use that kind of exposure and free advertising."

"You've got it! It's a deal." The two men shook hands again.

Everyone was excited and happy about the article and anticipating how the pictures would turn out. Would it be a close match to the portrait?

"Speaking of the article, Prudy, we have some work to do."

"Of course, but you know pretty much the entire story of Alexandra and the mayor. What else do you need?"

"Actually, I need some more information about the town in general and I have a few questions to ask you personally. Can we discuss this over lunch?"

"Sure, just let me get out of this dress. It's beautiful, but awfully warm. I'll get changed and then we can go. I know just the place, too. It's a restaurant in one of Mystic Port's beautiful, old historic homes that was turned into an inn, and you can see the harbor from there. It's quite a wonderful view."

"That sounds great."

Chapter Twelve

On the other side of town, which faced the ocean, the historic Mystic Port Inn stood majestically in all its magnificent glory. The old inn was a testament to the sheer architectural magnitude and stately elegance of Victorian style, with its enormous three floors, two turrets and beautiful stained-glass windows. As the couple pulled up in front of the hotel, Dylan appeared to be awestruck.

"Wow, now that's some inn. Is this where we're having lunch?"

"Yes, there's a restaurant on the first floor. And guess what it's called?"

Dylan scratched his chin. "Is it the Beaudicort Bar and Grille?"

"No, it's Alexandra's Allure."

"Well, I have to say, Alexandra is certainly well-known in this town."

"Yes, she is. There's no question about that. I think the notoriety has worn off a bit in the last several years. But with the town's anniversary coming up and your article, I think she'll be the talk of the town once again. I just hope they will view her in a positive light."

"You know what I think?" Dylan paused. "I think you'll both be the talk of the town. You look a bit uneasy, Prudy. Are you okay?"

"Yes, I'm okay, just a little bit concerned that the anniversary celebration, the article, and maybe even our investigation to get to the truth could possibly cause a problem with our unwanted house guest. But do you think a spirit or ghost that resides in a place, like our house, actually knows what's going on in another place like the museum or even here? Or maybe they can even transport to another location."

"I really don't know. I think that's probably a question for Dr. Spelling. Although, didn't he say he'd never come across that before? I think he said that spirits normally reside in one place. But then again, who really knows for sure?"

"I'm mostly concerned about Aunt Maggie."

"I can understand that, but we'll be careful about how and where we investigate."

Prudy led the way up the front steps to the magnificent Victorian mansion. Dylan opened the front door for her as chimes announced their arrival. A handsome waiter with startling red hair and a handlebar mustache greeted them.

"Good afternoon, Prudy. Would you like your usual table next to the side window?"

"Yes, please. I rather enjoy having a view of the old port while I'm eating."

"The young man led them to their table and gave them menus.

"What can I get you to drink?"

"I'd like an iced tea, Daniel."

"And for you, sir?"

"Make that two, Daniel. I'm Dylan, by the way."

"Pleased to meet you, Dylan. I'll be right back with your drinks."

Dylan grinned and scratched his chin. "Seems like everybody in this town knows you, Prudy."

Prudy laughed. "It's a small town, and when you have a deceased, notorious relative in your life, well...people are curious.

"I can honestly say that you have definitely piqued my interest. From the moment I first met you, I've been captivated."

Prudy blushed. "You're not so bad yourself, Dylan."

The friendly waiter returned with their drinks. "Do you need a few minutes to decide?"

"Oh gosh, yes, I didn't even look at the menu yet," Dylan said to the waiter.

Once they'd ordered lunch, Prudy suggested that Dylan ask any additional questions he might have so he could finish the interview, even though she secretly wished it would never end. She enjoyed being with Dylan and was worried that once the interview was completed that he wouldn't come around again.

"Okay, I'd like to know how you became interested and so knowledgeable about history and literature."

"That's easy to answer. Growing up in Mystic Port with all this history around me, and with my ancestors having settled here from France, I couldn't help but not be interested in history."

"Really? So, Alexandra and her husband were not the first relatives you know who lived in Mystic Port?"

"Yes, that's correct. My uncle, Samuel Beaudicort was the great grandson of Jean-Claude and Monique Beaudicort, who came here from France in the late 1700's to escape the French Revolution."

"Oh yes, I remember you mentioning a young couple who came here from France during our initial interview. So, they were relatives of Samuel and Alexandra and you, and your Aunt Maggie as well. I'd like to include that in the article. Family histories are always interesting. And what about your interest in literature?"

"That's an easy question to answer also. When you have an interest in history, you have to read a lot and do research. Plus, I also think reading just for pleasure is a great way to relax and be entertained. You can get away for a while without leaving the house."

"That makes sense. I have one more question. What ever happened to Alexandra's son, Simon?"

"Oh yes, poor, little Simon. I think about him often. Aunt Maggie told me that he went to live with Alexandra's cousin who raised him as if he were her own son."

"I see. That's good. I was worried about the poor, young fella, what with losing both his parents as a young boy."

"Yes, and he must have grown up, gotten married, and had his own family because here I am, a direct descendent of the Beaudicort family. My mother's maiden name was Beaudicort, but my father's surname was Trivit, in case you're wondering."

"Well, you answered all my questions, so I think I have pretty much everything I need, with the exception of the photograph of you."

And at that precise moment, Prudy's cell phone rang. It was Gertrude.

"Prudy, Ernie is back with the photos, and they're stunning. There's one in particular that's my favorite and my personal pick for the one I think Dylan should use with the article. But I'll leave that up to you two. If I hadn't seen him take the photograph with my own eyes, I'd swear it was a picture taken of the portrait of Alexandra."

"Really, that's fabulous! Dylan and I are having lunch at Alexandra's Allure, but we'll stop at your shop in about thirty minutes or so, after we've finished up here. See you soon. And please tell Ernie how much I appreciate his help in taking the photos and developing them so quickly."

Dylan's eyes were ablaze with excitement. "I take it the photos are ready?"

"Indeed, they are. All we have to do is finish our lunch, settle up on the bill and we can drive back to Gertrude's and have a look."

Chapter Thirteen

Excitedly, Dylan and Prudy charged into Gertrude's shop like a couple of teenagers going to pick up their prom pictures. No one was in the front of the shop.

"Gertrude, we're here," Prudy yelled.

Gertrude responded, calling them to come back to the study. When they entered the room they found Gertrude sitting on a fainting couch with a paper in her hand. She was shaking her head and appeared to be extremely distraught. Prudy approached her and put her hand on Gertrude's shoulder.

"What is it, Gertrude? You look quite upset."

"I...ah, I've been trying to get that top drawer of the desk open for months now and haven't been able to. Something was jamming it. So, while I was waiting for you two to get here I started fiddling with it. And I finally got it open."

Dylan asked in a rather confused tone, "So why are you upset?"

"I pulled out this old envelope and it had a letter inside. It was what was jamming the drawer."

"What does the letter say?"

Gertrude looked sadly at Prudy, then continued. "I know how fond you are of being Alexandra's niece. And I know you believed, as I did, in her innocence." She held up the letter. "But this was written by Alexandra herself as a confession. It's written right here that she had murdered her husband."

Prudy was now the one who looked upset and dejected. The color fading from her cheeks. "It can't be. It just can't!"

"Here dear, read it for yourself. I'm so sorry." She handed the letter to Prudy.

Prudy took it and sat down beside Gertrude on the fainting couch. She slowly read it.

June 25th, 1897~ I, Alexandra Beaudicort, being of sound mind and body, am writing this to inform the magistrate that I am guilty of the murder of my husband, Mayor Samuel Beaudicort. ~Alexandra Beaudicort

Prudy put the letter down beside her. She looked so distraught, Dylan just had to know exactly what Alexandra had written. He picked up the letter and read it. He paced around the room with it in his hand. He read it again, and then again.

"Prudy, you told me you have some letters Alex had written, didn't you?"

"Ah...yes, that's right. Aunt Maggie has quite a few letters in an old box that were written by either Samuel or Alexandra, why?"

"You told me during the interview that it had been rumored that Amelia Sanderson, the housekeeper, had committed the murder of the mayor, right?"

"Yes, but I guess I was wrong. It's right there in Alex's own handwriting," she said as she pointed to the letter Dylan still held in his hand.

"How do we know this letter was really written by Alexandra? We don't, do we? Consider this. If Amelia Sanderson wanted people to believe in Alex's guilt in order to take the suspicion off herself, maybe she wrote the letter and signed it as if Alex had written it."

Prudy hopped up from the couch. "You're right, Dylan! We have to go check those other letters and compare them to this one."

They turned to leave the study and were just about out of the room.

"We'll let you know what we find out, Gertrude."

"Aren't you two forgetting something?"

Prudy stopped short. "Forgetting something?"

"The photos Ernie took. Don't you want to see them and pick the one you think should be included in the article?"

Both she and Dylan looked at each other and then laughed.

"I can't believe we forgot. I mean that's why we came here. But you know, once I read that letter, every thought other than vindicating my dear, departed aunt left my mind, because I am still one-hundred percent sure of her innocence. Yes, please show us the photos."

"They're really quite something. I swear if I hadn't seen Ernie take the pictures with my own eyes, I'd bet the one on top was an original photo of Alexandra."

Gertrude got up from the chaise and walked over to the desk, picked up a large envelope and pulled out the photos, looking at them again, which caused her to smile, then handed them to Dylan. Prudy huddled beside him so they could look at the photos at the same time.

"Wow, the resemblance is uncanny. Prudy, you're a dead ringer for Alex." He handed the top picture, which was also his pick to go with the article, to Prudy so she could get a closer look.

"Gosh, this turned out beautifully. Ernie's a good photographer."

Gertrude laughed. "Yes, he is, but I believe the model had something to do with it too. Prudy, you're a natural. When this picture is published with the article Dylan's writing, well, you'll be a sensation."

"That's only if we can prove Alexandra's innocence."

Gertrude's expression became serious. "Let me run this by you. I also don't believe that Alexandra murdered her husband. I just can't accept that. No one else knows about this confession letter. Does anyone else really need to know?"

"Hmm...I'm not sure. But what I am sure about is that even though I believe in her innocence, I need to know the whole truth and exactly what happened," Prudy said in a serious tone. "In my heart, I believe she's innocent. But I want to be able to prove it."

Chapter Fourteen

"You two are lucky I brought that box of letters down from the attic a few months ago. Otherwise, we'd have to try to get into the attic again, which I'm not too keen about doing right now. Can I see the confession letter?"

Prudy handed her aunt the letter they'd brought back with them from Gertrude's shop. Maggie read the letter, shook her head, then laughed it off. She obviously didn't believe it was a real confession written by Alexandra.

"Oh, and you've got to see this, Aunt Maggie. Take a look at the photo Ernie took of me after I dressed up in Alex's gown and posed for him."

"Oh my goodness, dear. You're gorgeous, don't you agree, Dylan?"

"I certainly do," Dylan said with a sparkle in his eyes.

It was obvious to Maggie that he had feelings for her niece, and that made her quite happy. Prudy had a lot to offer the right young man, and she had a feeling Dylan Monroe might very well be Mr. Right.

"Aunt Maggie, how many letters in that box were actually written by Alex?"

"If I remember correctly, there's only one letter actually signed by Alexandra. There are more letters written by her husband, and even one note written by Amelia, the housekeeper."

Dylan's eyes lit up at the mention of Amelia. "Really, a note written by Amelia? That's exactly what we need."

Aunt Maggie looked at him quizzically. "I thought it was letters written by Alexandra you needed."

"Yes, we do, but you see, I'm of the basic belief that Amelia was the murderer and I think there's a very good chance she forged the confession letter to take the suspicion off her and back onto Alex. A written confession, I mean that would have carried a lot of weight with a jury, don't you think?"

"Indeed. I see where you're going with this. You'd make an excellent investigator, Dylan."

"Thanks, now let's go take a look at these letters."

"Come out to the kitchen, you two. I'll make a pot of coffee, and we'll sit at the table and study them."

Dylan and Prudy sat down, and each took a pile of letters and started to look through them.

"Gosh, there's so many letters in here. Every one of them I've looked at so far was written by the mayor."

"Me too," Dylan said as he carefully opened another folded and yellowed letter. He read it thoroughly and studied the signature. "Bingo!"

"You found the one written by Alexandra?" Aunt Maggie asked excitedly.

"Yes, and from what I recall the signature doesn't really look the same as the one on the confession letter. I believe it could be a forgery. Prudy, let me see that confession letter again."

"Aunt Maggie, I gave it to you, didn't I?"

"Yes dear, it's right here," Maggie said, as she turned to pick up the letter she'd placed on the counter while she made the coffee.

"Oh my God!" Maggie yelled as she saw the confession letter smacked right up against the coffee maker and saw it had already started to burn.

Dylan quickly crossed the room and picked up the paper by the top part that had not yet started to burn. Prudy grabbed the kitchen towel and quickly ran part of it under the faucet, then yelled for Dylan to put the letter in the sink. He dropped it into the sink, grabbed the dampened towel and blotted at the orange embers as they ran up the bottom of the paper.

"There, I think the fire's out." Dylan said as he gingerly picked up the paper and turned it over to look at the writing. He was horrified to see that Alexandra's signature was no longer visible on the paper that had burned to just above where it had been signed. "Oh no."

"What's wrong?"

"The signature was burned off."

Maggie sat down and hung her head dejectedly. "I'm so sorry. I'm usually very careful about using the stove or coffeemaker. I didn't think I put the paper so close to the coffeemaker. Now I've ruined everything."

"We don't blame you, auntie. Look, the window above the counter is open and the curtains are moving from the breeze blowing in. I bet the breeze blew the letter close to the coffee maker."

"But I still feel responsible."

Dylan put his hand on Maggie's shoulder. "It's really okay, let's just find that one letter you thought was in the box that was from Amelia. We can compare the handwriting."

The three of them searched through the letters again, but they did not find one that was from Amelia.

Prudy said, "You know, I think whoever the other spirit is, the angry one, who I believe is Amelia, doesn't want us to be able to prove Alexandra's innocence. It's possible Amelia's hiding the letter you believed was written by her that you thought was in the box so we can't compare it to the handwriting on the forged confession letter."

Dylan and Prudy sat wearily back down at the kitchen table. Prudy held back a yawn and said, "So where do we go from here?"

"Well, I guess that depends on you, Prudy," Dylan replied.

"On me? What do you mean?"

Maggie was listening intently to this conversation between her niece and Dylan, curious to hear what these two would decide to do next.

"What's important to you? Do you need to prove Alex's innocence, or will you be content in not really knowing for sure?"

"Oh, I know for sure. She's innocent. But what I'm concerned about is this article you're writing, my connection to Alex, and how other people will see it. I know she's innocent and I think Amelia's guilty, and I agree with you that she's the evil spirit that's causing all this trouble. The problem is, now how do I prove Alexandra's innocence?"

Dylan smiled and said, "Don't think I'm crazy, but how would you feel about a séance?"

"A séance? You mean right here in this house, and who would be in charge of a séance? Do you know of anybody who's conducted one before?"

Aunt Maggie suddenly spoke. "If you don't know of someone, I do."

"Really, Aunt Maggie? You know of someone who has experience in conducting a séance ?"

"Yes, she's a psychic medium by the name of Selena McNight. She's the friend of an old acquaintance of mine."

"I see. I think it's worth a shot. Aunt Maggie, how would you feel about having a séance here in this house?"

"I like the idea. It could be rather interesting. Besides, you might finally get the answers you're seeking about Mayor Beaudicort's murder and what exactly happened, and why. I'd bet money that is was Amelia Sanderson. But I also would like to know for sure why she murdered him. Was it because she was in love with him and he wouldn't comply? I do have one concern though."

"What is it, Aunt Maggie?"

"We'd want to communicate with the spirit of Alexandra. However, if we think the opposing spirit is Amelia and she resides in this house also, can we be sure we wouldn't get her?"

"I think I can answer that question," Dylan said. "I believe the medium focuses only on the spirit you're trying to communicate with. But you should check with the medium who would be conducting the séance . to be sure."

Prudy was excited about the prospect of holding a séance . "Can you get in touch with this acquaintance of yours, Aunt Maggie? If we're going to have a séance , I'd like to do it as soon as possible."

Dylan nodded in agreement. "Yes, the answers we seek, and what we may find out, could affect the article, although I'm aware we should approach the article from that standpoint delicately."

"Then I'll go make a call or two," Maggie said. "This should be quite interesting."

Chapter Fifteen

Selena McNight was a fifty-something, psychic medium and a friend of one of Maggie's old high school friends, Mabel Fenmore. She walked through the front doorway with a look of trepidation on her face.

Noticing Selena's apprehension, Maggie asked, "Are you sensing something already? You look a bit uneasy."

"No...no, but I'm almost expecting to, based on what you've told me about your discontented spirits."

Miss McNight slowly walked into the living room where Dylan and Prudy sat on the sofa, not knowing quite what to make of this rather unusual woman. They just smiled at her.

"Please sit down, Selena. Make yourself comfortable," Maggie said.

"Your antique furniture pieces are really lovely," Selena said as she chose the loveseat to sit upon.

"Thank you. You know many of these pieces belonged to Alexandra and the mayor."

"Really? They're beautiful and look to be well taken care of."

"Yes, Prudy and I feel quite fortunate to have inherited the house and many of these fine pieces of furniture and art. We can't thank you enough for coming over to meet with us here. I know you're a busy writer."

"Well, when I received your phone call last night, I could hear the concern in your voice. So why don't you tell me more about what's been going on here and what you're trying to accomplish with a séance."

"I'll let my niece, Prudy, tell you the story."

Prudy proceeded to tell Selena the entire story, about all the strange things that had happened since Dylan came to interview her, just a few days earlier. And about the hauntings and mishaps that had occurred over the last several years.

"So, basically what you're telling me is, you're hoping to find out from your dear, departed great, great aunt is that she's innocent and did not murder her husband, the mayor."

Dylan chimed in. "And we're hoping she can point us to some definite evidence, and ideally something that proves that Amelia was the murderer. So we'll know for sure."

"I see." Selena sat contemplating this seriously for several minutes. She finally said, "Okay, I think we can do this, but I'd like to do it soon. How about tomorrow evening when the moon is full?"

Dylan could not help but smirk.

Selena noticed the look on his face. "Listen, I know you probably think this sounds like a bunch of hocus pocus or mumbo jumbo, but as a spiritual and psychic medium, I feel my psychic abilities are keener during a full moon. It's really just as simple as that."

Prudy darted a serious look at Dylan. "Selena, yes, we'd like to go ahead and have you conduct the séance here tomorrow night. Is there anything you will you need us to do to prepare for it?"

"I would suggest having at least one more person present, maybe someone who knows the details about Alexandra."

"I could ask Gertrude and Ernie to come. Is there anything else we need to do?"

"Yes, this murder happened back in 1897, if I remember correctly, and Alexandra and the mayor actually lived in this house, is that correct?"

"Yes, this was their home."

"That's very good. When I hold a séance, I try to keep things as close to how they would have been at the time the event or incident occurred. Say for instance, in this case, we'd want to have candles or kerosene lamp light, no electric lighting.

"What room would you like to conduct the séance in?"

"We'd all have to sit around a table, preferably a round one. Do you have a round table?"

Maggie rather excitedly announced, "Yes, the antique, oak table in the kitchen is round and would be perfect. And it was the table they actually used when they lived here."

Selena smiled and nodded approvingly.

"Is there enough seating for all of us around the table?"

"There's seating for six. There will be five of us, maybe six if Gertrude's nephew comes too."

"Actually, I'd like to bring my friend, Albert Shoeman, along with me. He's also a psychic medium. The more open channels there are to the spirit world, the better. Do you have extra chairs, and do you think he could squeeze in?"

Aunt Maggie assured Selena they could all fit around the table and then asked if there was anything else she thought she'd require for the séance.

"If you have a picture of the person you're trying to contact, that would be good. Even better if you also have a personal possession of theirs."

"Oh, we have a picture of Alexandra and several of her personal belongings."

"Excellent! We'll have the séance in the kitchen tomorrow night at 10:00 p.m. on the dot." Selena quickly rose from the loveseat, smiled and walked towards the front door, then turned to add, "I'll be here at about 9:30 to prepare."

Maggie smiled at Selena, then asked, "How much will your services cost?"

"Nothing. I use the séances I conduct and any other psychic services I provide as research for my books. I'm a ghost writer," she said with a laugh.

Prudy muffled a giggle, not knowing if Selena was trying to be funny, and definitely not wanting to offend her in any way.

Maggie loved a good ghost story. "Oh, I'll have to read your books, Selena."

"I write under the pseudonym Raven Night and my books are available at all the major bookstores." And with that, she was out the door.

Aunt Maggie, Prudy and Dylan all stood there and just looked at each other. Maggie was the first one to break the silence.

"She's a bit of a character, isn't she? I can't believe we're going to have a séance here in this house. I don't know about you two but I'm a little nervous."

Dylan smiled at her. "We're all in this together. I'm hoping Alexandra will somehow tell us the truth about what happened when her husband was murdered and provide us with some kind of proof."

"Yes indeed," Maggie replied. "It would be good to know the whole story and finally put this ordeal to rest once and for all. But at the same time, it has been a bit exciting and intriguing."

Prudy smiled and looked at Dylan.

"It's certainly been intriguing, but a bit frightening at times also. I think we could do without the fires."

Maggie added, "I'd like to think Alexandra could finally rest in peace if she's vindicated."

Chapter Sixteen

It was a beautiful late summer evening. The full moon hung low in a partly cloudy sky and there was a light but blustery breeze. The brass bell wind chimes that hung from a strategically placed hook suspended from the eves of the porch, gently tinkled with each gust. The atmosphere was intoxicating, magical. Maggie and Prudy were waiting on the front porch for Dylan to arrive.

Dylan showed up at a little after 9:00 p.m., almost an hour before the séance would begin. Excited, he took the steps two at a time and joined the ladies on the front porch.

"Perfect night for a séance, don't you think?" he said with a smile. He leaned in close to Prudy who sat on a wicker loveseat. You look lovely tonight, Prudy."

"And you look rather handsome, Mr. Monroe."

"Thanks, I wasn't quite sure what to wear to a séance."

Maggie laughed and said, "I don't think it matters what you wear, but I agree with Prudy. You look quite dashing, Dylan. Now, if you two will excuse me, I have some snacks and beverages to prepare in the kitchen."

"We'll be in soon to help you out, Auntie."

"There's plenty of time before the others arrive. So, you two enjoy the fair weather this evening and that very romantic, full moon." Maggie winked at Dylan as she slipped in the front doorway.

Dylan sat next to Prudy on the white, wicker loveseat. "So, are you ready for the séance?"

"I guess so, if you can really be prepared for such a thing. How about you?"

"Me? Oh sure. It should be quite interesting. I am hoping that Alexandra will grace us with her presence and that we'll find out the whole truth about the murder. I'd like to finish writing the article for the newspaper, and I'd prefer to be able to write about her at least with the knowledge that she was innocent."

"Oh, me too. It may sound a bit strange, but Alexandra and I have had a connection since I was a little girl, and I know all the bad things that have happened are not because of her."

"So, you're quite sure the murderer was Amelia?"

"Yes, I've always believed that."

"And do you think she's the bad spirit who has been haunting you?"

"I believe Amelia has been haunting us at the house, yes. But I also know for sure that Alexandra has made her presence known at the house as well."

"Are you scared of what might happen at the séance?"

Prudy took a deep breath and sighed. "Scared? Not really. Maybe a little bit nervous. But ultimately, I believe in the triumph of good over evil, so I'm thinking positively."

Dylan gently ran his fingers down Prudy's jawline. "That's my girl."

Just at the moment when Prudy found Dylan staring into her eyes and she thought he might kiss her, a car drove up in front of the house. Prudy recognized it as Gertrude's car. Ernie was in the passenger seat and waved to Prudy as Gertrude parked the car.

Once parked, Gertrude and her nephew quickly walked up the front steps. "Goodness, we're not late, are we?"

Dylan was amused. "Late? No, you're actually a bit early. Miss McNight and her friend aren't due to arrive for about half an hour."

Prudy smiled at Gertrude and Ernie. "You two can go on in if you'd like. I'm sure Aunt Maggie would like to see you, and I'm sure she could probably use your help getting things set up."

Ernie looked a bit longingly at Prudy. "Aren't you coming in?"

"Yes, Dylan and I will be along in just a few minutes."

Ernie walked through the front doorway, allowing the screen door to "accidentally" slam behind him.

"I think I may have some serious competition," Dylan said as he touched Prudy's chin and gently tilted her face so she'd look directly at him. "Could that be a possibility?"

Prudy laughed nervously. "Ernie? He's harmless."

"I wouldn't be too sure about that. What is it they say? You have to watch out for the quiet ones. I think Ernie may have a thing for you."

"Oh, don't be ridiculous! I've known Ernie since grade school. Besides, he's not really my type."

"Am I your type, Prudy?" Dylan asked as his look became serious, and he gazed deeply into her eyes.

Prudy responded to Dylan's gaze and tilted her head just a bit. Dylan pulled her close, then again touched his hand to her face, running his fingers along her jawline. As his hand stopped at her chin, he gently tilted her head a bit more, then touched his lips to hers.

The warmth of his lips and being so close to Dylan caused Prudy to feel a bit light-headed. She also never wanted the moment to end. Suddenly, a blustery breeze started to blow, and a shiver ran down her spine.

"Oh, Prudy, you're shivering. Here, take my jacket."

"No, that's okay. But it's nice to know that chivalry is not dead. Maybe you could put your arms around me to keep me warm."

"Gladly. Now, where were we when we were so rudely interrupted?"

"I believe we were in the middle of a kiss when Gertrude and Ernie pulled up."

Dylan pulled her close and they kissed. After the kiss ended, Dylan said, "I'm sure this night will be one I won't ever forget."

Prudy smiled. "Me, neither. But I'm sure Aunt Maggie could use our help now."

"Yes, of course. But are you okay? You look a bit flushed. You haven't seen a ghost, have you?"

"No, not yet. But I do hope to later. I guess it's just the affect you have on me, Dylan."

Prudy stood up and headed towards the door, then paused and turned to look directly at Dylan. "And by the way, the answer is yes."

"Yes?"

"Yes, you are most definitely my type."

Chapter Seventeen

Selena McNight entered the candlelit living room looking every bit like a textbook model of what a spiritual medium should look like. Her jet-black hair was pulled tightly back; wavy tendrils cascaded around her face. Deep green eyes sparkled in the candlelight; her excitement was palpable.

"I'd like to introduce you to my friend, Albert Shoeman. Albert is a close friend of mine and he's also a psychic medium."

Albert Shoeman was a pudgy, short, bald man with heavy, black-rimmed glasses with lenses that were so thick that his eyes appeared magnified, like a bug's. He said in a rather high-pitched tone, "It's a pleasure to meet everyone."

Maggie introduced Gertrude and Ernie to Selena. Gertrude was quite excited to meet Selena.

"I believe I've read every one of your books, Miss McNight, or should I call you Raven?"

"I'd prefer if you called me Selena. Raven Night is my pseudonym . I only use it for my books."

"Of course, Selena. It's a pleasure to meet you. And you as well, Albert."

Albert took Gertrude's hand and squeezed it. "The pleasure is all mine." Gertrude now appeared a bit nervous and giggled nervously like a schoolgirl.

Once all the introductions were completed, Aunt Maggie suggested they all go into the kitchen. "Please follow me and come this way everyone. We're all set up for the séance in the kitchen."

The group of six followed Maggie. The kitchen was rather dark, the only light coming from some candles and a dim light from an oil lamp that sat on the antique oak desk beside the pantry doorway. Maggie offered her guests some mulled cider and passed around a plate of spiced wafer cookies.

Everyone sat around the large, oak table. Selena waited until all the guests had finished their cider and cookies.

Selena then took over. "Is everyone ready for me to begin?"

"Yes, I believe everyone is ready," Maggie said.

Maggie, do you have some of Alexandra's belongings?"

"Yes, here are a pair of gloves and a small purse that belonged to Alexandra. Will that be enough?"

"Yes, those will be perfect," Selena said as she took the items from Maggie and put them on the table in front of her. "Everyone, please pay close attention to my instructions. It's extremely important that we do this correctly if we want to have a successful séance. And I believe that is something we all would like to see happen for Maggie and Prudy. Now, please place both of your hands palms down with your fingers spread apart on the table in front of you, touching the tips of your thumbs together. The tips of your little fingers should be touching the tips of the little fingers of the person sitting on either side of you. Once you have done that, then I'll begin. I must request that no matter what happens, please try not to break the circle. That's very important. If we break the circle, Alexandra will probably not make an appearance tonight. Also, I am the only one who should be speaking during the séance. Do you understand?" Everyone nodded in agreement.

Dylan whispered in Prudy's ear. "Here we go. This is it."

Selena gave Dylan a sharp look which he took as a warning that whispering would also not be tolerated. He nodded at Selena and then she started the seance.

"We are gathered here this evening to call on the spirit of Alexandra Beaudicort, wife of the esteemed Mayor Samuel Beaudicort." She continued to say the name Alexandra over and over again, in a slow, even chant. This went on for several minutes.

"I beseech you, Alexandra, to give us a sign. Are you here, Alexandra?"

Nothing.

Please, Alexandra. Your great niece, Prudence is here. You are among friends in the very home where you lived. We wish you no harm. We seek only the truth."

A cool breeze flowed into the kitchen through the open window. Prudy shivered and shifted in her chair. Selena continued her chant.

The breeze became stronger and caused the curtains to billow up and out. All the lit candles in the kitchen flickered, and then all but one went out. Everyone at the table took that as a definite sign that Alexandra was making her presence known. She was there!

All the participants in the séance were fixated on Selena, waiting to see what would happen next. Everyone, that is, with the exception of Prudy. In the darkened room, no one noticed that her eyes were closed, and her breathing had become heavy and deep.

Suddenly, there was an eerie silence in the room. The breeze stopped, but instability hung heavy in the air. The temperature dropped dramatically. Everyone turned their gazes from Selena to Prudy, who had started moaning.

Aunt Maggie moved with the intention to stand, thinking she had to help her niece, that maybe something was wrong with her. But Selena, who felt Maggie's hand move, stopped her. Selena whispered to Maggie. "I believe it's Alexandra coming through Prudy. Please don't break the circle."

Prudy started to speak, but it was not her voice. It was a deeper tone than Prudy's. Everyone stared at her as she spoke. Albert's eyes, behind those thick-lensed glasses appeared as if they'd pop right out of his head, as he looked at her in total shock.

"This table...I can't look at it. This is where she prepared his lunches to take to the office. I can't bear to look at it!"

Selena asked softly, "Alexandra, please tell us why you can't look at the table."

"It's...it's where she made the salad, the one that he ate before he...he...she poisoned him!"

"Who poisoned him?"

"Amelia! Amelia Sanderson poisoned and murdered my dear husband, Samuel. I loved him so."

"Alexandra, do you know why she killed him?"

"Yes, she wanted him all to herself. She was in love with him, a sick and twisted love, and when she couldn't have him, she...she killed him."

"Alexandra, we desperately want to exonerate you. There are people in this town that believe you were the murderer."

"That's not true! I loved Samuel."

"We know it's not true. We know you're not a murderer. But do you have any proof that Amelia committed the murder?"

"Yes, she came to see me in jail, and she told me that she did it. She said if she couldn't have him, then nobody could. And she laughed in my face." Prudy started to cry.

Maggie was visibly shaken but Selena continued.

"I'm sorry, Alexandra. Tell me, please, is there any proof, like a written confession or anything? We want to vindicate you."

"She forced me to write a confession letter. She told me if I didn't write it and sign it, that she'd hurt my sweet, little boy."

"I understand," Selena said softly. "But is there any proof that you didn't murder your husband or a confession made by Amelia?"

"No...no, except for..." she paused.

"Except for what?"

"Amelia kept a journal"

"Alexandra, do you know where the journal is now?"

Prudy slowly raised her hand and pointed to the antique oak desk that was beside the pantry doorway. Everyone turned to look where she was pointing.

Maggie said softly, "I've never been able to open the top drawer of that desk. It's been locked for as long as I've lived here and I don't have the key. We can't open that drawer without it."

"Dylan said in a quiet tone, "We'd have to destroy the desk to get to the contents in the drawer."

Selena looked quite agitated and whispered loudly, "Silence!"

Maggie looked distraught at the thought of having to destroy the antique desk to get inside. But she was willing to do so if that was the only way they'd be able to see what was inside and discover if among the contents they'd find Amelia's journal.

Everyone gasped out loud when they heard the sound of something metal hitting the wood floor. Selena slowly got up and rubbed her fingertips back and forth on the floor in the area where the noise had come from. She stood up and whispered loudly, "I got it, It's a key!"

Suddenly, Prudy came out of her trance and grabbed Dylan's arm.

Selena said, "I thank you Alexandra for coming through to us tonight. We will now close the circle."

Dylan hugged Prudy. "You're okay, Prudy. I'm right here with you."

"Dylan, what happened?"

"The séance is over."

"Oh...right, the séance."

Prudy tried to stand up but Dylan told her to stay in her seat.

"You should stay where you are for a few minutes, Prudy. Take your time, there's no rush. Maggie, could you get Prudy a glass of water?"

"Yes, of course."

Chapter Eighteen

"Prudy, are you sure you're okay? You look flushed." Maggie asked as she handed her niece a glass of cold water.

"Yes, I'm okay. I just feel kind of tired and drained."

"But you don't remember what happened during the séance?" Dylan asked her.

She looked at Dylan, her expression serious; the look in her eyes was one of pleading. "No, I don't remember a thing. Please tell me what happened. Did we get an answer as to what actually happened and who murdered Mayor Beaudicort?"

Selena sat down beside Prudy at the table. "It appears that your Aunt Alexandra was compelled to come through you, dear."

Dylan added excitedly, "It was like you were possessed."

Selena continued. "Well, basically speaking, she was temporarily possessed by the spirit of Alexandra."

"And what did I say, or do?"

"You told us that you, or Alexandra actually, were innocent of the murder of her husband." Selena moved in closer to Prudy and added in a quieter voice, "And you told us that Amelia was the murderer."

"I knew it! But what about proof? Is there any proof?"

Dylan explained that Alexandra told them that Amelia had a journal, and when Selena had asked her where it was, she pointed to the antique desk by the pantry.

"But that drawer has been locked forever, and we've never been able to find the key," Prudy said in a frustrated tone.

Selena went on to explain the strange phenomenon of the key that seemingly fell out of the air and hit the floor.

Dylan added, "It was really freaky. I guess the key has been somewhere in this house for a long time, and Alexandra knew where and gave it to us."

"Well, what are you waiting for? Dylan, try to unlock the desk drawer!"

Selena handed the old, metal key to Dylan. A thin, shredded, purple ribbon was tied through the open, filigree top of the key. He went over to the desk and slowly put the key into the keyhole of the drawer. He slid the key into the keyhole as he smiled at Prudy.

"Go ahead, try to turn the key and open the drawer," she said impatiently.

Everyone held their collective breaths as Dylan slowly turned the key. They could hear grating as the key turned in the lock. Then there was a click, finally unlocking the drawer that had been frozen in time for possibly the last one hundred years or more. He slid open the drawer and peered inside. He saw nothing. There was nothing in the drawer.

"Pull it out further. I think I see something in the back, right corner of the drawer!" Prudy said with a shrill excitement in her voice.

Dylan reached toward the back of the drawer and gently pulled out a small, but rather thick journal. He examined the leather-covered journal and then placed it on the kitchen table in front of Prudy who, after running her fingers over it, gently picked up the journal and opened it.

Everyone gathered around her at the table. Dylan sat closely next to her. "You know we're going to have to go through each and every page until we find the one where Amelia writes about Mayor Beaudicort. Are you up for that Prudy, or are you too tired from the séance?"

"Oh, I'm up for it alright. There's no way I've come this far and then I couldn't possibly wait until tomorrow to see the truth written in her own words. There's no way I could fall asleep tonight not knowing the truth. The anticipation would kill me."

"You're not the only one," Dylan added.

Prudy gently and slowly turned the yellowed and brittle pages, thinking it was going to be quite a slow process, then soon realized the pages were dated. She would just have to find the journal entries for 1897.

But what exact date should she be looking for?

"Dylan, when you were interviewing me that first day, I looked up the exact date of Mayor Beaudicort's death, right?"

"Ah yes, you did. Why?"

"These pages are dated. Do you remember the date I told you? I believe it was in June, but I don't remember the exact date. I guess I could just read through every page in June, 1897.

Dylan scrunched up his face and tried to recall what Prudy had told him during the interview and shook his head. "No, I'm sorry but I don't remember."

"Not a problem. Do you have your tape recorder handy?"

"Yes, I do have my recorder and that tape, the one I used when interviewing you. It's out in the car. I'll go get it. I'll be right back!"

At this point everyone was sitting again at the table, all much too involved to even think about leaving, despite the late hour. Just as the clock struck midnight, Dylan returned with the small tape recorder in his hand. He sat back down next to Prudy and turned on the recorder. He pressed the button to rewind, and after several attempts, finally found the part of the tape from the first day he'd interviewed her.

Everyone listened intently as they heard Prudy talking about the mayor's death, and could hear her leafing through papers, and then saying, "Here it is. Samuel Beaudicort died on June 15th, 1897." Dylan snapped off the recorder.

Prudy was already leafing more quickly through the old journal until she found the entries written during the month of June 1897. Aunt Maggie couldn't help herself and yawned.

"Oh, please excuse me. It's the hour, not the company or the subject matter, I assure you."

"It won't be too much longer. I think I'm almost at the right entry, Aunt Maggie."

After she carefully turned a few more pages, Prudy finally found Amelia's journal entry for June 15, 1897. She read quickly with Dylan leaning in against her, as he tried to read the entry at the same time.

Prudy gasped as she read Amelia's admission of guilt. Selena was becoming impatient. "Prudy, please tell us. What does it say?"

Prudy read the entry aloud:

"I loved him. I would have done anything for him. But he told me he loved his precious Alexandra, and I knew he would never leave her. So, I did what I had to do. The foxglove worked much more quickly and more effectively than I thought it would. The Magistrate has Alexandra in custody. She will be jailed and awaits a trial. She's where she belongs. If it had not been for her, I'd have everything. June 15, 1897, A"

Prudy gently put the journal down on the table and looked at Dylan, who had leaned back into his chair and appeared content in the knowledge that what Prudy believed to be true all along had indeed been the truth. He looked at Prudy and smiled.

"Well, now you finally have your proof. Have you thought about whether or not you're going to make this proof public knowledge?

Maggie looked apprehensive. "I'm not sure that would be such a good idea.

Prudy hesitated. You know, I agree with Aunt Maggie. Dylan, I don't think it would be a good idea for you to include anything about the journal entry in your article."

"It's completely up to you. But are you sure you wouldn't like everyone to know the truth once and for all and put an end to the public scrutiny about you and your family?"

Prudy slowly stood up and paced the kitchen. "It was important to me that Alexandra's innocence be proven, but I know what Aunt Maggie is concerned about. I'm also concerned. There are people in this town, descendants of Amelia Sanderson, who would not like us proving Alexandra's innocence by exposing Amelia's guilt. I'd be afraid of the repercussions."

"So how do you want me to handle this as far as the article is concerned? Like I said, I'll leave it entirely up to you."

Prudy sighed heavily.

"Listen, it's late and you don't have to decide what you'd like to do right this minute. There's still a little time before the article must be published. I know it's a serious matter for you and for your aunt to consider."

"Wait, I think I have an idea. How about this? Do you think there is a way you could write the article and say something about there being recent evidence that points to Alexandra's innocence, but not write explicitly what the evidence is and without implicating Amelia?"

"Sure, I could do that, and actually I think it's a good idea. But then I do hope that everyone who has been a party to this séance, and to what is written in this journal, will agree to make no mention of it to anyone."

Selena asked each person in the room if they would agree to not mention the séance or the journal to anyone outside of those in attendance. Everyone agreed.

Chapter Nineteen

Although exhausted, Prudy couldn't sleep. She was either thinking about the séance and what had occurred, or the goodnight kiss that she and Dylan shared out on the front porch, before he left after the séance. He'd promised her that he'd write the piece for the newspaper in a way that she would approve of and insisted that with the accompanying photo of her dressed as Alexandra and posing as she had for the portrait, that she, Prudy, would be the talk of the town. No one would even be thinking about Alexandra's guilt or innocence. She smiled to herself as she thought about their conversation.

"Oh, I really don't have any desire to be in the limelight, Dylan."

"You know, there could be so much interest in this story that you could write a book, Prudy."

Prudy laughed. "I don't fancy myself as a writer."

"But I am a writer. You could tell the story, and I could write it. We could collaborate and possibly have a bestseller on our hands. What would you think of that?"

Prudy laughed, then gave Dylan a playful, little shove. "Yes, let's do it!"

She'd had to admit she really liked the idea. Besides, it would give Dylan and herself a reason to continue to work together, and that idea pleased her very much. She told Dylan she wanted to discuss the details more, but that she would like to go ahead and plan to do it. Writing a book about Alexandra would be the perfect tribute to her dear departed aunt.

Finally, Prudy fell deeply asleep and dreamed. She had a vivid dream about Alexandra, who entered Prudy's room by floating right through the closed door, and she appeared to hover at the foot of the bed. She had on the beautiful gown from the portrait.

"Aunt Alexandra, it's so good to see you."

"Prudy, my dear. I came to thank you."

"Thank me, for what?"

"For believing in my innocence all these years, even before you saw the evidence and proof."

"Yes, I've always known you were innocent, Aunt Alexandra, but it took Dylan to help me prove it."

"He is a fine, young man. He reminds me very much of my husband, Samuel. He even looks like him. He's a keeper, Prudy. I have a feeling you and he will write a fantastic book together and will form a partnership that will last a lifetime. It's meant to be."

"I'm glad for your support, Aunt Alexandra."

"Of course. And I'm always looking out for you, you know. By the way, you looked stunning in my gown. That photograph will cause quite a stir, as will the article. I see wonderful things in your future, dear. I must go now but know that I am always with you in spirit."

Just then, Prudy awoke. She blinked and looked for Alexandra but then realized it must have been a dream. But she also knew that spirits of loved ones often came to people in dreams. Prudy closed her eyes again. She slept like a baby for the rest of the night. All seemed well and right.

The next morning, Prudy joined her Aunt Maggie at the kitchen table. Maggie had already poured Prudy a cup of steaming, freshly brewed coffee.

"Good morning, dear."

"Good morning, Auntie. How are you feeling this morning? Did you sleep well?"

"As a matter of fact, I did. I slept like a baby until 8:00 a.m. this morning. It's almost as if the spirit of angry Amelia is gone. Do you think that's possible?"

Prudy slid into a kitchen chair and hugged her coffee mug with her hands. "You know, I do think that's possible. Now that Amelia's spirit knows we've found proof that she was the murderer, she may have finally decided to give up her evil hauntings once and for all."

"Oh, I do hope so. It would be nice to have some peace and quiet around here again.

"I agree. I have some good news for you, Aunt Maggie," Prudy said happily.

"Good news?" Maggie sat down across from her niece, extremely interested in what this good news might be.

"Dylan and I are going to write a book together about Aunt Alexandra."

Maggie's voice resonated with delight. "That's a super idea! Will it be the true story about Alexandra or a fiction story but based on her life?"

"We haven't gotten that far yet. We're meeting for lunch to discuss the details. I'm really excited about the project and the prospect of working with Dylan. I was afraid that since he had everything he needed for the article, that I might not be seeing as much of him."

"Dear, I truly believe he would have found some way to keep seeing you. I've seen the way he looks at you. There's a sparkle in his eyes. And I know you're very fond of him. I think the idea of you two collaborating on a book is fantastic. I'm thrilled for you."

"That's what Alexandra thought too."

Aunt Maggie almost choked on a mouthful of coffee. "What did you say?"

"Alexandra came to me in a dream last night. She thanked me for believing in her innocence all these years, even before I actually saw the proof. And she already knew about our book idea. She told me she had a feeling we'd write a fantastic book together."

"I'm so happy for you, dear." Maggie smiled warmly at her niece. "Now, what can I make you for breakfast?"

"Oh, I appreciate the offer, but I think I'll just skip breakfast this morning. I'll be meeting Dylan shortly."

Maggie sat down at the table while Prudy drank her coffee.

"So, the anniversary celebration weekend is in three weeks. Will Dylan have the article finished by then?"

"Oh, I'm sure he'll have no problem getting it finished. He told me that the most time-consuming part is getting the information for an article. Once he has that, the actual writing is easy for him."

"I'm so excited to read it, and for the anniversary celebration. The town has been all a buzz about it most of the summer. It should be quite exciting."

"Which reminds me, I'm hosting the gala ball at the museum on the Saturday night of the weekend celebration. I really haven't made any definite plans yet. Sheesh, I have a lot of work to do in a rather short amount of time."

"I'll be more than happy to help in any way I can, Prudy. Just say the word."

"Oh, thank you, Aunt Maggie. I don't know what I'd do without you."

"Have you thought about what type of gala it will be?"

"Yes, I'd like it to be an affair just like they would have had back in 1897. I contracted Gilbert Tyler's band to play in the ballroom, and I envisioned dancing and candlelight. The members of the historical society will all be there dressed in late Victorian garb. But I will need to hire a caterer for seating and light refreshments. And I'll also need to hire someone to decorate in the ballroom."

"I bet Gertrude would love to do that for you. She's great at that kind of thing."

"Yes, Gertrude does have a flair for that. She did all the decorations at the town hall for Christmas last year. It was gorgeous! I'll stop by the shop and ask her if she'd be willing to do the decorations for the gala."

"I'm positive she'll say yes. She likes being involved in the community. And she really loves you, Prudy."

Prudy finished her coffee. "Well, I'd better get a move on if I'm going to get anything done today." She arose from her chair, gave her aunt a peck on the cheek, and then she went back upstairs.

After Prudy had showered and dressed, she took special care while applying her makeup and styling her hair. She wanted to look her best for Dylan.

Chapter Twenty

Dylan sat at the same table at the Mystic Port Inn where he and Prudy had dined previously, eagerly awaiting for her to arrive for their lunch date. The waiter gave him a menu to look at while he waited. He perused the lunch selections and then turned the menu over to read the history of the Mystic Port Inn on the back cover.

The Mystic Port Inn, circa 1860, is the former home of the Sanderson family.

He turned to look when he heard the door open and beamed at Prudy as she entered the dining room. He stood to greet her and pulled out a chair at the table for her. "As always, you look beautiful, Prudy."

Prudy slid into the chair. "Thank you, Dylan. Hey, are you okay? You look kind of weird, like you've seen a ghost or something."

"Well, funny you should say that. Just as you were coming in I read this," and he handed her the menu with the back cover towards her so she could read it. "Did you know this establishment was the Sanderson's residence years ago?"

"Yes, of course I do. I am the town historian you know. But I don't understand why that would bother you, Dylan."

"Well, I'm just a bit concerned that the ghost of Amelia Sanderson might be here, aren't you?"

"No, I've been coming here for years and never had anything unusual happen. Besides, until the séance last night and the proof we found that she murdered Samuel, I'm pretty sure her spirit had taken up residence at our house, not here."

"I wonder if a spirit or ghost can move around to different places. I mean, in light of recent events I'd be worried she might have just relocated here."

"I truly don't think there's anything to worry about, Dylan. I really don't. I have a feeling we won't be seeing or hearing any more from her."

Just then the waiter came over to the table. "Are you ready to order, or would you like some more time?"

Prudy smiled. "I didn't read the board when I came in. Are there any specials today?"

"Yes, we have a California summer chopped salad with fresh greens, avocado, tomatoes, goat cheese, and crispy noodles. The soup of the day is butternut squash. Oh, and we have a French Dip sandwich today also."

"They all sound good but I think I'll go with the California chopped salad and a cup of the butternut squash soup.

"And for you, sir?"

"You know, I think I'll have the same thing."

"And how about your drinks?"

"I'd like iced tea please."

"And for you, sir?"

"I'll have the iced tea as well."

"So Dylan, let's talk about the book. How will we decide whether to make it a non-fiction, factual book about the history of Mystic Port and Aunt Alex, or a fictional paranormal mystery?"

"I've been thinking about that. You know we have such an interesting and good story here. I was thinking it should be a fiction, but based on the true story, and we can even state that in the beginning of the book."

"You mean like an introduction?"

"Exactly. What do you think?"

"I agree, but I think the introduction would be rather lengthy if we really explained the facts as they occurred."

"I don't think that should be a problem. One thing I've learned as a journalist is to edit and cut things down and still get the point across."

"Yes, I'm sure you do. I've been wondering, how and when will we start the process of writing the book?"

Dylan smiled and gently touched Prudy's hand. "It's going to require a lot of weekends and evenings together, if you're up to the task."

Prudy returned the smile. "Yes, I'm up for it and I won't be thinking of it as a task. Actually, I'm so excited to do this that I can hardly wait to get started!"

"I think it might be a good idea to wait until after the anniversary celebration, so we can give this book our complete and full attention. Your plate is awfully full right now. But I'd like to mention the book in the article, to put it out there and draw attention and interest to the fact that we're writing a book about the events surrounding Alexandra, the mayor's murder, etc. And with that in mind, we should think about a title."

"Oh yes, a title."

Just then, the waiter brought out their drinks. "Sorry this took a few minutes. Tina wanted to brew some fresh tea for you."

"Not a problem," Dylan said, and then looked quizzically at Prudy. "That wouldn't be Tina, your assistant, would it?"

"One and the same. Tina works part-time in the kitchen here. She's a college student trying to earn a decent salary. She also rents a room here."

"I see, interesting," Dylan said, scratching his chin.

A few minutes later the waiter brought out their soup and salads.

"Oh good, I'm really famished," Prudy said, as she enthusiastically dove her fork into the salad.

Just then, Tina stuck her head out of the kitchen door. "I hope you two enjoy the salads," she said with a grin. "I made them especially for you."

"I'm sure they'll be fantastic, Tina," Prudy called to her, just before she was about to put her fork in her mouth.

Tina watched as Prudy tried her salad, obviously waiting to get the thumbs up sign from her.

"This is delicious, Tina. What's the dressing you used?"

"It's an avocado and creamy peppercorn mixture. Do you like it?"

"I think it makes the salad."

"Glad you like it. How about you, Dylan?"

"I'll let you know. I'm eating the soup first, while it's hot."

"Enjoy, you two." she said with a grin and then disappeared back into the kitchen.

Dylan leaned forward and said in a whisper, "In light of the fact that a salad was the method by which Mayor Beaudicort was murdered, and considering how Tina feels about us, maybe ordering a salad wasn't such a great idea. I'm checking for foxglove leaves and flowers in my salad before I eat it. Also, I've been wondering, could Tina possibly be related to the Sanderson family?"

Prudy laughed.

"No, I know Tina's mother quite well and I know they're not related to the Sandersons. Actually, Tina's mother rather dislikes the Sandersons. And Dylan, Tina does not dislike us. The way she acts, that's just her. She's a bit immature, and honestly, I think she has a bit of a crush on you."

Dylan laughed.

The couple talked about the town's anniversary, the gala ball, the article, and their book as they ate lunch. They finished their meals and asked for their check. Dylan paid the entire bill, including the tip.

"Dylan, thank you. But I wasn't expecting you to pay for my lunch."

"It's my pleasure, Prudy. Besides, we were discussing the article and the book, so it's a legitimate business expense," he said as he gave her a wink.

Dylan pulled out Prudy's chair for her and the couple headed towards the door to leave. Tina stuck her head out of the kitchen door again.

"Have a nice day, you two. And don't get into any mischief. Keep your eyes on the sky so you'll be prepared for any stormy weather. You don't want to be caught off guard!"

Dylan turned back to look at Tina. "Now what makes you think we'd get into any mischief," he asked with a grin.

"Well, I've seen it happen before. When you two are together, strange things happen."

"See you, Tina."

"Goodbye, Dylan."

Prudy and Dylan walked out to the front porch of the old inn.

"See what I mean? I'm telling you she has a crush on you. You'd better be careful."

"No way. She's a mere teenager."

"I'm serious, she has a thing for you."

I'm sure she'll get over it. Next week she'll have a crush on the UPS guy or something. So tell me, what are your plans for the rest of the afternoon?"

"Well, I've just got to go over to Gertrude's shop and talk to her about the ball. It's in three weeks and I'm not nearly as organized as I should be. I'm going to ask Gertrude if she'll take care of the decorations and the catering for me. She's great with that sort of thing, very organized."

"I'm sure she'll love doing that for you. She really seems to be quite fond of you, Prudy. Listen, do you mind if I tag along?"

"Of course not. I'd love the company. You know it's such a gorgeous day and the shop isn't that far. We could walk there."

"Sounds great. Let's go."

Chapter Twenty-One

Gertrude, busy in the back of the shop, turned when she heard the bells on the front door as it opened. She smiled and walked to the front of the shop when she saw who it was.

"What are you two up to on such a beautiful day?"

Prudy smiled warmly at Gertrude. "We just had lunch at Alexandra's Allure and then walked here to see you. I have a favor to ask you."

"Well ask away, dear. What can I do for you?"

"You know the gala is in just three weeks. And I couldn't think of a better person to be in charge of the décor and catering for the gala than you, Gertrude. Now, before you decide, let me give you the details and tell you what would be involved. First of all, I have a budget for the gala, and you would not be paying for anything out of your own pocket. The gala will be taking place at the museum in the ballroom. You'll have free reign on the décor. The only thing is that I'd like it to look like it's 1897."

"Oh, that is right up my alley, Prudy. I'd be thrilled to do that for you. Have you hired a band? Are the invitations taken care of?"

Dylan took the opportunity to look at the vintage clothing in the shop.

"Oh, where are my manners?" Gertrude asked. "Please come, you two, and let's sit down in the back where you'll be more comfortable and we can discuss this further.

"That's okay, Gertrude. I was just looking for something to wear to the gala. I'm hoping to be Prudy's date if she'll accept my request to escort her. Do you have any men's clothing from that period?"

"Yes, I do, and I have some of the mayor's things also. I believe you and he are probably about the same height and build. And wouldn't that be exciting? Prudy will be dressed in Alexandra's beautiful ballgown and you in the mayor's tuxedo. You'll make a handsome couple, and you'll end up being the talk of the town. I'll show them to you in just a moment, Dylan." Gertrude focused back on Prudy.

"So dear, are the invitations already taken care of?"

"There won't be any invitations sent out, Gertrude. There's going to be an announcement in the paper next weekend and the weekend before the gala, and tickets will be sold at the museum and library up until the Friday before the gala. There are 248 tickets available. First come, first serve.

And you and your guest won't need a ticket, of course."

Gertrude nodded in approval. "That's a good way to handle it, Prudy."

"And much less costly too."

"I'm so excited about this. I'll start working on the details first thing Monday morning."

"Great, and thanks, Gertrude. You have my cell phone number if you have any questions, and you can come to the museum, which will be available to you anytime during regular business hours. But if it gets down to the wire and you need to be there after hours or weekends, just let me know."

Prudy gave Gertrude a hug.

"Now, about those clothes, Dylan. Let's go back and have a look."

Dylan approached Prudy and touched her hand. "I didn't mean to be so forward in assuming I would escort you to the gala. Will you do me the honor, Prudy?"

Her eyes sparkled. "Yes, of course I will. I was already counting on you being my date."

Dylan beamed as he locked eyes with Prudy. Gertrude smiled at the couple.

"Are you coming with us to the back to see the mayor's clothing?"

"No, that's okay. I'll stay up front here and look at the jewelry," Prudy replied.

Dylan followed Gertrude to the back room. Prudy took her time and looked in each of the jewelry display cases. She spied a gorgeous citrine necklace that must be at least one hundred years old. She bent down to see if she could read the price. She groaned when she saw the price was over two hundred dollars.

Just then Dylan and Gertrude came back into the front room.

"What were you groaning about?" Dylan asked.

"Oh, nothing really."

"What were you looking at? Did something catch your eye?"

"Well, I do love the citrine necklace in there, but I was just looking really. How did you make out with finding a suit?"

"We found the suit that was Mayor Beaudicort's, the one Gertrude thought would work. It's a tuxedo. She just has to make an alteration to the length of the sleeves of the jacket. But it will be ready in plenty of time for the gala."

"Oh, good. I bet you'll look quite handsome in it."

Prudy turned to Gertrude and thanked her again. "I'm sure we'll be speaking and meeting several times in the next few weeks."

"You're very welcome. I'm really enjoying being able to help you out and being a part of what I'm sure will be a very momentous occasion."

Dylan and Prudy headed for the door to leave the shop. They stopped in their tracks as two fire engines, sirens blaring, sped up

Main Street headed west, in the direction of the Mystic Port Inn.

Gertrude approached the now open door and peered outside. "Here comes another one. It must be a serious fire. I hope no one is hurt."

Prudy was always concerned at the thought of a fire, especially after so many had occurred the previous summer at her and her aunt's home. "Well, at least they're not going in the direction of my house, this time."

"Good thing." Dylan said, although he had a serious expression on his face. "Why don't you give your Aunt Maggie a call, just to make sure she's okay anyway."

"Good idea." Prudy called her aunt who picked up on the first ring."

"Hello?"

"Hi, Aunt Maggie. I'm just calling to check in with you because I've been gone a bit longer than I had anticipated."

"I'm fine, dear. But there must be a pretty big fire somewhere in town because I keep hearing sirens, a lot of them."

"Yes, Dylan and I are just leaving Gertrude's shop, and three fire engines went by, west on Main Street. We have to walk back that way because Dylan and I left our cars at the inn and walked here after lunch. I'll let you know if we see anything."

"Yes, please do. I hope no one gets hurt."

"Me too, auntie. Goodbye."

Dylan impatiently tugged on Prudy's sleeve. "Come on, Prudy, let's go."

The couple walked quickly in the direction that would take them back to the Mystic Port Inn, Dylan holding Prudy's hand and almost pulling her along like a child at times.

"Why are we hurrying?" Prudy gasped.

"Our cars are parked near the Inn. I'm just hoping the fire isn't there, or near, our cars. Come on, Prudy!"

As they got closer they could see thick, black smoke and smell the acrid stench of burning plastic and rubber. Prudy choked.

"Look, it's the Inn!" Dylan yelled. "And my car is scorched! We shouldn't get any closer. It's not safe. If cars are on fire, there could be explosions."

"Oh my God," was all Prudy could manage to say.

"I hope everyone got out of the Inn okay."

"Oh my God, Tina." Prudy stood close to Dylan, who put his arms around her to comfort her.

"What time is it?"

Dylan looked at his watch. "It's just after 2:00, why?"

"Tina only works at the Inn on the days she's there until 2:00 p.m.," Prudy said as she scanned the area around the Inn, stopping to focus on a group of people behind a barricade on the other side of the building, opposite to them.

"There she is in that crowd of people standing behind that barricade. And the head chef and the waiter who served us lunch are there too."

"Oh, that's good. I'm glad they got out safely."

"Your car looks pretty bad, Dylan. I'm so sorry."

"Well, I'm not thrilled about it, but it's just a car, and besides, I have good insurance. Looks like your car was untouched. Good thing you parked on the street."

"Yes, lucky for me." Prudy noticed a new look of concern on Dylan's face. "What is it? What's wrong?"

"I left my briefcase in the car. I had a lot of my notes for work in there."

"If your briefcase burned up, you won't lose everything for the article, will you?"

"No, it's all on my laptop computer and luckily I didn't bring it along today."

"Good thing."

They stood for several minutes watching the firemen douse the old inn until the smoke finally stopped from pouring out the windows, and after several minutes they realized that they could no longer see any flames or smoke from the building or Dylan's car.

"Looks like the firemen did a good job putting out the fire, Prudy."

"Yes, but the Inn looks like it's in pretty bad shape. Such a shame. It's one of the town's oldest, historic buildings."

Dylan hugged Prudy. "Yes, it is a shame, but the important thing is that it looks like no one was hurt." He kissed her gently on the cheek. "Come on. Let's go see how bad my car is."

Chapter Twenty-Two

Just two days after the fire at the Inn, Dylan pulled up to the Mystic Port Museum and Library in a rental car and parked right in front of the building. He jumped out of the car, walked around it, opened the front passenger door and grabbed his new briefcase. He quickly shut the door and locked the car, then bounded up the front steps of the library.

Prudy had just stepped out of the main entry doorway to put up the "open" sign. "You certainly are here bright and early, Dylan."

Dylan was all smiles. "I'm not going to let something like a fire and a destroyed car dampen my spirits. Besides..."

"Besides...what?"

"The article's finished."

Prudy stared at Dylan and then smiled. "Really?"

"Yes, I wouldn't lie to you about something so important, Prudy." He gazed at her and slowly moved in close to her. "I never would have been able to write this article without you. You were...are my inspiration."

He moved even closer to her. "I think I've found something very special here in Mystic Port. When my boss first gave me this assignment, my initial reaction was...boring. But now I realize I'm one lucky journalist, and man."

This proclamation by Dylan moved Prudy deeply. "I'm glad you were given this assignment too. You've brought a dimension of excitement and passion to my life that I never realized could exist, Dylan." Prudy smiled at him. "So how long are you going to keep me in suspense?"

"What do you mean?"

"About the article. Can I read it please?"

"Oh, yes, of course. That's why I brought my laptop."

"And I hope you have saved copies of the article."

"Of course. Let's go into the library so you can sit down and read it. I'm excited to see what you think."

Dylan held the door for her and entered the museum room behind her. They quickly walked through the museum to go to the library, but Dylan slowed as he passed Alexandra's portrait and gazed at it as he walked by. He could not seem to be in that room without stopping to look at the portrait. Every time he looked at it he was awestruck by the incredible beauty of Alexandra, and by how very much Prudy resembled her beautiful aunt.

"Come on, Dylan!"

He quickened his step and followed Prudy into the library, to one of the big, carved library tables where they each took a seat. Dylan quickly pulled his laptop out of his briefcase and opened it and turned it on. He clicked on the article and pushed the computer over to Prudy so she could read it. "Here you go. I really hope you'll like it."

Prudy read the article stopping occasionally to smile up at him, or to laugh at one of Dylan's anecdotes. Once she'd finished reading, Prudy sat back in her chair and sighed.

"What is that sigh for? Don't you like the article?"

"No, to be honest I don't really like it." Prudy hesitated for effect, and then blurted out, "I love it!"

Dylan laughed. "You had me going there, you little vixen."

"Who, moi?"

Dylan shook his head and smirked. "Yes, you. We really need to celebrate the completion of the article, you know. But I have to go back and return to the office today and start working on a new project."

The smile suddenly left Prudy's face. She hadn't really thought about what would happen when Dylan had finished with the article. She felt rather foolish. After all, he did have a job to return to.

Dylan stood up, walked over to Prudy, put out his hand and pulled her to her feet. He pulled her close.

"Prudy, don't look so sad. Newport is not that far away. I'll be back on the weekends, and we will be talking every day on the phone."

"Do you promise?"

"Now how can we write a book together if we don't talk or meet to discuss things?"

Relieved, the smile returned to her face.

"That's my girl. Now, I've got to take this finished article to work, have my editor do her thing, and wait for it to be published in the paper the Sunday before the gala. I'll bring you the advance copy so you can see it before anyone else in town. I know one thing for sure."

"What's that?"

"That this was the best assignment I've ever had, and that you, young lady, are going to be the talk of the town."

Dylan smiled and looked into Prudy's eyes. "Thank you, Prudy."

"Thank you, Mr. Monroe."

Just as they were in the middle of a rather impassioned kiss, the door to the library flew open, and like a tornado, in flew Tina.

"Hah! I caught you! Tina said, in between snaps of her gum.

The couple broke apart.

"Good morning to you too, Tina," Dylan said in a sarcastic tone. He backed slowly away from Prudy but continued to look at her longingly.

"Well ladies, work calls, so as they say in France, adieu. Prudy, I'll call you this evening."

Prudy watched as Dylan put his laptop back in his briefcase and left the library, but not without turning and smiling at her one last time and giving her a wink before he walked out the door.

"Well, it looks like our Prudy has herself a boyfriend," Tina said mockingly.

Prudy turned to look at Tina disapprovingly. The girl always managed to annoy her with her immature and insensitive remarks. But Prudy was determined not to let anything, or anyone, ruin her elation.

"Yes, Tina, it would appear you're correct." And with that, Prudy walked right by Tina to her desk to work on the details for the gala.

"Please make sure you index and put the new shipment of books in the right places in the library. They've been sitting here since last week."

"Yes, ma'am! Tina said and then snapped her gum as loud as she could before she turned to walk away.

"Oh, and one more thing, Tina."

"Yeah, what's that, Pru?"

"You know the rule the board has about no gum chewing in the library. You could literally destroy a book with gum, in which case you would lose your job and have to pay damages."

Tina grimaced, then turned to grab the box of books Prudy wanted indexed and placed on the shelves.

"Tina, before you even think about opening that box, get rid of the gum!"

"Yes, ma'am!"

Chapter Twenty-Three

The days seemed to fly by as Prudy worked diligently on the plans for the 250th Anniversary Celebration and Gala. The weekends were mostly spent with Dylan. They worked on the book they were writing together, went out for dinner, to the movies, and sometimes stayed home at Prudy's playing Gin Rummy with Aunt Maggie, who'd grown even fonder of Dylan, and the idea of him and her niece being together and in love.

One Friday afternoon, Prudy received an unexpected phone call from Ernie.

"Hello, Ernie. What can I do for you?"

"I'd like to ask you if you'd allow me to be your escort for the gala."

Prudy had always been rather fond of Ernie and didn't want to hurt his feelings. She did some quick thinking and came up with what she thought was a brilliant idea.

"I appreciate that, Ernie. But as it turns out, because he wrote the article and everything, Dylan will be escorting me to the gala. But you know my assistant, Tina, will be attending and I know she doesn't have a date yet. I think maybe you should give her a call."

"Oh, Tina, is she the pretty blond I sometimes see in the library?"

"Yes, she's the one. Like I said, I know for a fact that she doesn't have a date yet and I'm pretty sure she'd love to have you escort her."

Ernie gladly took Tina's number.

After she'd gotten off the phone, Prudy laughed and thought how clever she was, trying to fix Ernie up with Tina. The more she thought about it, the more she liked the idea. They'd actually make a cute couple. And neither of them was dating anyone. Yes, it made perfect sense.

When she got home, as they often did before dinner on a Friday evening, Prudy and Aunt Maggie sat and had a glass of wine together. Prudy told her aunt about her call from Ernie and what she'd suggested to him.

Maggie laughed nonstop for a good fifteen seconds.

"What's so funny, Aunt Maggie?"

"It will be like the spitfire and the geek, that's all. It could be dangerous."

"Well, they do say opposites attract."

"I guess we'll find out if that's true or not, won't we?"

Prudy joined her aunt in the laughter, and the two of them were giddy, almost in tears when they heard a knock at the screen door.

"That must be Dylan," Prudy said, as she got up to unlock the door.

Dylan walked into the living room and smiled at Prudy, then nodded at Maggie. "How are you ladies this beautiful evening?"

Maggie burst into laughter again.

Dylan acted like he thought Maggie was laughing at him. "What, is it something I said?"

Maggie, still laughing and unable to speak, shook her head in the negative.

"Actually, I heard you ladies laughing it up from outside. Have you two been drinking wine?"

Prudy looked at him sheepishly. "Yes..."

"Well, aren't you going to offer me a glass?"

Maggie got up and headed for the kitchen. "You two sit down and relax. I'll get Dylan a glass of wine." And she continued to laugh all the way out to the kitchen. "Don't have too much fun without me!"

Dylan sat next to Prudy on the sofa. "Seriously, what was so funny?"

She explained about the call from Ernie and told Dylan what she had suggested about Ernie escorting Tina to the gala.

"Now that could be dangerous!"

In walked Maggie with the glass of wine for Dylan. "That's what I said!"

"The idea is rather humorous, you know." Dylan said as he started to laugh, which caused Maggie and Prudy to start laughing all over again.

Finally, after a few minutes, the laughter finally subsided and they started to discuss the actual details of the gala and what a great night it was going to be.

"Prudy, are you all set? There's only a week to go until the big event."

"Yes, Dylan, especially with Aunt Maggie's and Gertrude's help. Things are pretty much under control."

Maggie added, "Prudy's been working almost non-stop."

"Yes, it does seem like I've been working like crazy. But I'm lucky that I have my job at the museum and library and can work on the details for the gala during regular business hours. Of course, I've had to give Tina some of my regular work, but she is my assistant."

"You know, the article will be in the Sunday edition."

Prudy stared at Dylan. "Did you bring the advance copy?"

"Yes, of course. I promised you I would. I have it right here," he said as he grabbed his briefcase. "All safe and sound." He pulled the newspaper out of his case and handed it to her.

She sat quietly and looked at the article and gazed at the picture of the portrait of Alexandra in the museum that was placed next to the photo Ernie had taken of her. While looking at the photos side by side, Prudy was amazed at how much she really did look like her great aunt, and by how the pictures looked almost identical. It was like a photographer had taken a picture of Alexandra when she was posing for the portrait.

"Well, don't keep me in suspense," Maggie pleaded. "Please let me see it."

Prudy handed the newspaper to her aunt, who was thrilled with the article and the pictures. "This is excellent work. And I like how the announcement for the gala is right under the article to draw attention to it. I bet there won't be a ticket left by Monday evening."

"Yes, that was brilliant thinking," Prudy said as she beamed proudly at Dylan.

"I have another surprise for you, Prudy. Something else that I'm hoping will please you."

Prudy looked at Dylan inquiringly but didn't say a word. Dylan pulled a small, gift-wrapped box from his briefcase. He handed it to her. "Here, this is for you."

"What is this?"

"You should unwrap it and find out."

Prudy unwrapped the box and removed the lid. Inside the gift box was a deep blue velvet jewelry box. She opened the velvet box and was stunned when she saw the beautiful antique citrine necklace she had been ogling when they were in Gertrude's shop.

"Oh Dylan, it's gorgeous. I just don't know what to say."

"You don't need to say anything. But there's more. There's a very interesting story behind that piece of jewelry. When I went back to Gertrude's shop to purchase the necklace, she wanted to clean it up before she wrapped it up for me to give to you. When she was cleaning it, she discovered something inscribed on the back of the citrine setting. Take a look."

Prudy took the necklace out of the velvet jewelry box and looked on the back of the beautiful citrine setting. She read the inscription that was in the shape of a circle out loud:

"To A From S ~ Je Vous Aimerai Toujours"

"I'm afraid my knowledge of the French language is not what it used to be. What does it say?"

Dylan smiled and said, "I will always love you."

Aunt Maggie stood up. "Can I see the necklace, Prudy?"

"Of course."

Maggie, with a quizzical look on her face, closely examined the necklace and the inscription. "I can't recall, is Alexandra wearing a necklace in the large portrait in the museum?"

Dylan smiled. "Possibly, but remember, her mouth and neck are not visible because of the fan she's holding. I do know she isn't wearing a necklace in the other painting, the one next to the portrait."

Prudy stood up excitedly. "Yes, but Alexandra is wearing a necklace in our portrait, the one in the dining room!"

The three of them quickly went out to the dining room and stood staring at the one portrait of Alexandra that hung over the fireplace. And there it was. She was wearing the beautiful citrine necklace.

Prudy said excitedly, "I can't tell you how many times I've sat here at the dining room table studying these paintings and I never noticed the necklace. You know how you're so used to seeing something that after awhile you don't really notice the details anymore?"

"Yes, exactly," Maggie said, then added, "It's strange though, that out of all the beautiful antique jewelry Gertrude has in the shop, that you were so taken with that particular piece. It's like you were meant to have it, Prudy."

Dylan smiled. "That's exactly what I thought. And Gertrude knew you'd love it."

"Thank you, Dylan. I can't tell you how much this gift means to me. I will treasure it always."

Aunt Maggie added, "Dylan, what a thoughtful and beautiful gift. It will look perfect with the gold gown. It makes me wonder if Samuel purchased the necklace for his wife with that in mind.

Chapter Twenty-Four

Dylan stopped by Prudy's house on the Thursday evening before the gala so he and Prudy could practice their ballroom dancing. Prudy found a recorded piece of music from the period of 1897, which was what the band performing at the gala would be playing. After practicing for almost an hour, the couple decided they needed a break. They went out to the front porch and sat closely together on the porch swing.

"I think we can pull this off, don't you, Prudy?"

"Sure, I think we'll be just fine. A glass of wine before we leave the house on Saturday evening might not be a bad idea, to loosen me up a bit."

"You'd better make sure you have a bite to eat too, or that wine could really go to your head."

Prudy laughed, remembering how the three of them had been drinking wine before dinner the previous Friday evening, and how she and her aunt had gotten a bit giddy. "Yes, I'll definitely heed your advice about that."

Dylan laughed. "I'll be picking you up at 6:30 p.m. on Saturday. Will Aunt Maggie be coming with us?"

"No, I believe she'll be there ahead of us helping Gertrude with any last minute preparations."

"You know, it will be just like I'm Mayor Beaudicort escorting his beautiful wife, Alexandra, to the Mayoral Ball." Dylan was staring into Prudy's eyes. "I feel very lucky to be the man escorting you to the gala."

Prudy returned the gaze and looked deeply into Dylan's eyes, and at that moment she knew beyond a shadow of a doubt she had fallen in love with this man. He was the man she had longed to find. He was that special someone she had only previously dared to imagine. Dylan was that special man who shared the same passion for history, literature, and art that she did. Not to mention he was interested in helping her find out the truth about the mayor's murder and Alexandra, something she had always been passionate about.

Dylan put his hands on Prudy's shoulders and drew her closer to him. His lips touched hers and he kissed her. Dylan stopped so he could tell her something that he felt needed to be said. Again, he gazed deeply into her eyes. "Prudy, I love you."

"Oh, Dylan. I love you too." And they kissed again but were forced to stop as a car came to a screeching halt in front of the house. It was Ernie, who jumped out of the car and leaped up the front steps two at a time. He was smiling broadly and was obviously excited and happy. Prudy, who was used to Ernie being so straight-laced, had never seen him this way.

"Hey guys! How are you doing this beautiful evening?"

"We're doing great, Ernie. How about you? What's up?"

"I just had to stop by to tell you that I did it. I got up my nerve and asked Tina to go to the ball with me on Saturday, and guess what?" And without giving either of them a chance to answer, he added, "She said yes!"

Dylan stood up and grabbed Ernie's hand and shook it. "Good job, my man."

"Thanks, Dylan. And thank you, Prudy."

Prudy winked at Ernie. "You two will make a wonderful couple, I just know it."

Dylan added, "Ernie, you'd better brush up on your ballroom dancing. The girls love that you know."

"You know, I may just do that. Well, I'll be on my way, but we'll see you on Saturday night!"

Dylan smiled and said, "You can count on it."

Ernie was back in the car and drove away quickly. Prudy chuckled, obviously quite satisfied with herself that she'd made the suggestion to Ernie, and that Tina had said yes and agreed to go to the gala with him.

"Well, young lady, it looks like your plan worked. I do believe there is magic in the air."

"Yes, I believe you're right, Mr. Monroe."

Dylan pulled Prudy to her feet. "May I have this dance, Miss Trivit?"

"You may, sir."

They went back into the house and practiced dancing for another twenty minutes until Prudy complained her feet were sore and she was tired.

"I'd better go, Prudy. I have to work tomorrow. And I guess you do too."

"Yes, I do."

She walked Dylan to the door, and they kissed good night.

"The next time we see each other will be when I pick you up on Saturday night for the gala. I'm really looking forward to it."

"Oh, me too. I'm excited. I'm glad we practiced dancing. I'd hate to get out there on the dance floor and make a complete fool of myself."

Dylan finally tore himself away from Prudy after a final kiss and walked in the direction of his car, but stopped, then turned and said, "Until Saturday."

Prudy smiled and waved from behind the screen door.

Chapter Twenty-Five

After all the planning and anticipation, the weekend of the 250th Anniversary Celebration and Gala had finally arrived. All the tickets for the gala had been sold and after all the hours of planning and hard work, the preparations were complete. The entire town was abuzz and excitement filled the air.

Prudy woke up early on Saturday morning and felt as giddy as a schoolgirl on Christmas morning. She took a shower and washed her hair, then slipped on a pair of shorts and a tee shirt. Her anticipation had been growing all week, especially after Dylan had given her the gift of the citrine necklace to wear with Alexandra's gown at the gala.

The knowledge that the necklace had once been given to Alexandra by Samuel, her husband, as a token of his love and admiration for her, made the gift particularly special. The fact that Dylan had given it to Prudy as a gift made it absolutely priceless.

Prudy's cell phone rang, and she saw that the call was from Gertrude.

"Good morning, Gertrude."

"A good morning to you, Prudy. I just thought I'd call to ask you if you'd like me to come over late this afternoon to help you with your hair. I have to drop the ball gown off anyway. I had it professionally cleaned for you."

"Oh, could you? I'm so glad you called. I've been having serious doubts that I could do my hair by myself and have it look like it does in the picture. And thank you for getting the dress cleaned. I hadn't even thought about that."

"Of course, I'll do your hair for you. What time should I be there?"

"Well, I think about 5:00 o'clock would be good, if that's convenient for you."

"Yes, five o'clock will be just fine. And then Maggie and I will head over to the museum to make one final check that everything will be ready for the ball."

"I can't thank you enough, Gertrude, for helping me out with the arrangements. I could never have pulled this off without your help. You're a life saver, really."

"It's been my absolute pleasure. You know, your mom would be so proud of the beautiful and accomplished woman you've become. It warms my heart to be able to help you. Especially since your mom is no longer here. You're like a daughter to me, Prudy."

Prudy was deeply touched by what Gertrude said and thanked her again. "You're an angel. Both you and Aunt Maggie are angels. I don't know what I would have done without you two. And not just with the plans for the gala, but how you and Aunt Maggie have always been there for me. After both my parents died, I was devastated. But Mom passing so soon after my father…"

"Of course you were devastated, dear. We all were, but especially you. You were at such a delicate, young age. Maggie and I were so concerned about you. But you have grown into a beautiful woman, one I am proud to call my friend. You overcame every obstacle that was thrown at you. Both of your parents would be proud of you. I'm sure they're smiling down on you, Prudy."

"Thank you, Gertrude. Your saying that means so much to me. It really does."

"Of course, it came from my heart. So dear, I'll see you this afternoon."

"Yes, indeed. Goodbye, Gertrude."

Prudy sat down at Alexandra's dressing table and looked in the timeworn mirror. She picked up the citrine necklace once worn by her aunt. She ran her thumb over the citrine, then turned it over and reread the inscription.

"To A From S ~ Je Vous Aimerai Toujours"

Prudy felt compelled to put the necklace on, even though she wouldn't be getting ready or dressing in the gown for several hours. She placed the necklace around her neck and fastened it. As she stared into the mirror, she became mesmerized. The timeworn glass of the mirror was a bit wavy and cloudy, and after looking at herself in the mirror for a few moments, Prudy became slightly disoriented, and when she glanced at her reflection in the mirror, she swore she saw the face of her great aunt smiling back at her.

The antique dressing table was next to the open window, and Prudy could hear the rustling of the leaves from the trees as a breeze suddenly stirred. The wind chimes on the porch below tinkled gently.

But there was another sound she could vaguely hear. It was like a whisper over and over again. Prudy looked back in the mirror, and to her utter amazement, Alexander's face had masked her own reflection and her lips were moving. Prudy was stunned by what she saw, but she was not afraid. She concentrated on the faint sound and the movement of the lips in the reflection in the mirror and finally heard it more clearly.

"*Je vous aimerai toujours,*" she heard in a whisper, hardly discernible from the movement of the leaves moving in the breeze outside. Then, the whispering stopped. Prudy shook off what she thought she'd heard, thinking she was overly tired from all the excitement of the last few weeks and about the celebration and gala.

She reached up and touched the citrine. Then she removed the necklace and put it back on the dressing table. The newspaper picture she had of Alexandra that had been partially secured in place behind the frame of the mirror, fell onto the dressing table. Prudy put it back in its place. She and Gertrude would be using the picture later to compare and make sure Prudy's hair and overall appearance matched that of Alexandra's in the picture.

Prudy glanced at the clock. She had a few hours before Gertrude would arrive to help her get ready and she was feeling a bit hungry, so she ventured downstairs and joined her Aunt Maggie in the kitchen.

"Good timing, dear. I just put the kettle on. Would you like to join me in a cup of tea?"

"I'd love to, Aunt Maggie, but I don't think we'd both fit."

Maggie giggled. "Oh, Prudy, you are funny! Seriously though, would you like a cup of Assam tea? Or perhaps you'd prefer your favorite jasmine green tea."

"Yes please, I'll have the Assam and I think I'll have some cheese and crackers also. I'm a bit famished." Prudy headed for the refrigerator, but Maggie sidestepped her.

"You sit down, dear, and let me take care of getting your snack. After all, you have a big evening ahead of you. Besides, I'm so excited I feel like I have to be doing something."

"Okay, Aunt Maggie. Gertrude called me a few minutes ago. She'll be here at five o'clock to deliver the gown and to help me with my hair. She had the gown cleaned.

Isn't she a dear? Then I guess you two will be heading over to the museum."

"Yes, Gertrude is a gem of a friend. What time will Dylan be picking you up?"

"He said he'd be here at six, but you know how he's always early."

"I think there's probably a good reason for that, dear. I think it's because he can't wait to see you. Could it be that he's fallen in love with you?"

Prudy became a bit flushed.

"Oh dear, I hope I haven't overstepped. I don't mean to be intrusive. I have just never seen you as happy as you've been these last few weeks. And Dylan is a wonderful young man."

"Aunt Maggie, of course you haven't overstepped. You're the only person I'd tell this to…Dylan told me he loves me, and I told him that I loved him too."

Maggie hugged her niece. "I couldn't be happier for you, dear."

Prudy sat down at the table and smiled as she watched her aunt make the tea and prepare a snack plate for them both. Once she'd gotten everything prepared, Maggie placed a serving plate of cheese and crackers, a teapot, and two teacups on the table and sat down across from Prudy. She then filled both of their cups with the hot amber liquid.

"There we go, afternoon tea. You know your grandmother, and your mom and I used to have afternoon tea together almost every Sunday afternoon. Actually, this teapot was your grandmother's. It's beautiful, isn't it? Brings back so many wonderful memories made right here in this kitchen, at this very table."

"It is very beautiful. Maybe you and I should continue the tradition and have afternoon tea every Sunday. We could invite Gertrude. She's practically family anyway."

"That's a splendid idea! I think we should do it."

The two ladies slowly drank their tea and finished the crackers and cheese. Maggie cleaned off the table and washed the dishes. Prudy helped her aunt by drying them. She yawned several times.

"Prudy, I think you better go up and take a nap before Gertrude arrives to help you with your hair. You've been going twenty-four/seven for several weeks. You look a bit tired, and you have a big night ahead of you." Maggie looked at her watch. "You have a couple of hours before she'll get here."

"You know, I think I will. After all, I want to look and feel my best tonight. If you don't hear me up and about by four, could you please wake me up?"

"Yes, of course, dear."

Prudy lay down on her bed and listened to the soothing sound the wind chimes made as the breeze gently caused the lace curtains to billow and sway in the open window beside her bed. She thought about Dylan and wondered if he was as excited as she was. She anticipated what the evening would be like and imagined dancing with Dylan, the two of them dressed to the nines, dancing the waltz they had practiced. She fell asleep with a smile on her face.

Meanwhile, Dylan had a really busy morning. He went to the barber shop and had his hair cut and then drove to Mystic Port to Gertrude's shop to pick up the tuxedo that she'd altered so it would fit him perfectly.

"I also had it cleaned for you, Dylan. You two are going to look wonderful and just like you stepped out of the 1890's."

"Thank you, Gertrude, for everything."

"Are you kidding? It's been my pleasure. To be honest with you, I've had more fun getting ready for the gala than I've had in a long time. I'm also glad Ernie has a date and will be attending. He seems happy. I was a bit worried about him before. I think he was lonely. But you have befriended him and now he has a date for the gala. I think things are looking up for Ernie."

Dylan smiled at her. "I'm glad too. It should be a night we'll all never forget. So, I'll see you this evening."

"Yes, you will. Don't be late!"

"Thanks again, Gertrude."

"Oh, Dylan, one more thing. I almost forgot. There's something I found in the pocket of the tuxedo jacket. After the jacket was cleaned, I put it back in the pocket where I think it's probably been for over a hundred years. Don't look at it now. Wait until you get home. I think it's something you'll find very interesting, and I think you'll know exactly what to do with it."

Dylan had an inquisitive look on his face. But he knew that Gertrude must have a pretty good reason for asking him to wait to look at whatever was in the pocket of the tuxedo jacket.

"Okay then, I'm very curious but I'll wait to look until I get home."

As he drove, Dylan imagined how beautiful Prudy would look in Alexandra's ball gown. He smiled to himself as he envisioned the two of them gliding around the dance floor.

When he arrived home, he ran up the steps with the garment bag to his apartment. Although he was eager to see what it was that Gertrude had found and put back in the pocket of his tuxedo jacket, he decided to wait just a bit longer. When he looked at his watch and saw that it was just after 4:00, he decided he'd better get a move on and get ready first. He only had an hour and a half before he had to be dressed and ready to leave to pick up Prudy. He quickly grabbed the newspaper and stared at the picture of her. His lips curved into a slight smile as he daydreamed about her. He thought about their future together and about the book they were writing. Everything with her had just seemed to be right and had fallen so easily into place.

Dylan took a shower, shaved, and then took the tuxedo out of the garment bag. He checked the pocket of the jacket and pulled out a velvet covered jewelry box. Dylan opened the box and examined the piece of jewelry. He smiled and felt compelled to call Gertrude to thank her. They talked for several minutes. After their conversation, he put the jewelry box back into the jacket pocket. He got dressed and checked himself out in the mirror. He smiled approvingly as he realized he could definitely pass as Mayor Beaudicort. And how stunningly beautiful Prudy would look on his arm, dressed in that gold gown looking very much like Alexandra. He was certain it would be a night they'd remember for the rest of their lives. There was magic in the air. Like a gentle electric current, it was palpable. He wondered if Prudy felt it too. He'd soon find out.

Chapter Twenty-Six

Gertrude stood behind Prudy as she examined herself in the mirror. "You look stunning, so beautiful, Prudy! And I know I must sound like a broken record at this point, but you look exactly like Alexandra does in the portrait in the museum. It's really quite remarkable."

Maggie stood over to the side in the doorway. She wiped a tear away. Overcome, her voice was shaky. "You are gorgeous, dear. How I wish your dear mother was here to see this. She would be so proud."

Prudy rushed over to give her aunt a hug. "Thank you so much, Aunt Maggie. You look beautiful yourself in your gown. Both of you look exquisite, like you just stepped out of 1897. You know I could never have pulled this off without your help. I want to thank you, both."

The three ladies couldn't contain their excitement. When the doorbell rang, all three of them exclaimed in unison, "That must be Dylan!"

Maggie said excitedly, "Gertrude and I will go down and let Dylan in. Give us a good two minutes, and then you come down,

Prudy. I think you should make a grand entrance. But be careful on the stairs. You're not used to wearing a long gown. I don't want you to trip and fall."

"Okay. You ladies should be careful too. Take your time on the steps."

Maggie and Gertrude carefully went down the stairway. The doorbell rang again. Maggie yelled excitedly, "We're coming!"

Once the two ladies were downstairs and eager to see Dylan in the vintage tuxedo, they both hurried to the door, and Maggie quickly opened it.

Dylan stood there with a quizzical smile on his face, peering inside, undoubtedly hoping to see Prudy. "Good afternoon ladies. I know I'm a bit early. May I come in?"

Maggie exclaimed, "Dylan, you are dashing in your tuxedo. Of course, please come in. She stepped aside to let Dylan in. "Please go into the living room and have a seat. Prudy will be down in just a minute."

Gertrude couldn't believe her eyes. Dylan's resemblance to Mayor Beaudicort from the pictures she had seen was astounding. She'd noticed he had a resemblance to the man previously, but the tuxedo sealed the deal.

"Thank you, ladies." Dylan winked at Gertrude. "You two look beautiful."

Dylan sat down but quickly arose when he heard a rustling noise coming from the top of the stairs. He stood there; his eyes fixed on the stairway anxiously waiting to see Prudy.

As she came into view, the three of them gasped in unison. Prudy looked magnificent. Although the two ladies had already seen her in the gown, the way Prudy almost floated down the stairs smiling at them, and Dylan's reaction to her stunning beauty, caused them to be overcome with emotion.

Dylan rushed to the bottom of the stairs, and as Prudy reached the last step, he offered his hand to her. She smiled at him and put her hand in his. "Prudy, you look absolutely stunning." Dylan then bowed and kissed the back of her hand. "I saw that in a movie once and always wanted to do it but never had the occasion to until now."

Maggie rushed to grab her camera. She snapped several pictures of the happy couple. Then she said to Gertrude. "Gosh, Gerty, we have to get to the museum, don't we?"

"Indeed, we do! We better get going."

On their way to the door, Gertrude turned. "Don't be late you two," she said as she winked at Dylan.

Aunt Maggie added, "We will see you at the museum in an hour. The ball will begin promptly at seven o'clock when you are expected in the ballroom on the dance floor, dancing the first waltz together."

"Okay, Aunt Maggie. Don't worry, I promise we won't be late!"

The two ladies left and finally the couple were alone. Dylan turned to look again at Prudy, his eyes taking in every detail of her form. "The necklace looks perfect with that gown, Prudy. I mean it, you're stunning."

"Thank you, Dylan." Prudy reached up and touched the citrine stone on the necklace. "I've never received such a beautiful gift, and one that means so much to me. I get goose bumps when I think about the fact that this lovely necklace once hung around my Aunt Alexandra's neck, and that she wore this gown. I feel like I'm living in a dream."

Dylan led Prudy over to the sofa. "Can you sit without wrinkling your gown?"

"I think I can manage if I'm careful," Prudy responded as she cautiously sat down on the sofa. Dylan sat closely beside her, he too, being careful so that he wasn't leaning against or crushing any of the fabric of the gown. He appeared somewhat nervous, and Prudy thought it was because he was worried about having to dance in the ballroom in front of all those people.

"Would you like to practice dancing again to the music the band will be playing tonight?"

"No, I don't think so. I'm feeling pretty comfortable about that. Not unless you think you need to, Prudy."

"No, I'm feeling pretty comfortable about the dance too. I just thought you seemed uncommonly nervous or anxious,

Dylan. I just figured it was because you were worried about having to dance in front of all the people who will be at the gala."

Dylan gazed into her eyes. "The truth is, Prudy, that I am a bit nervous. But it's got nothing to do with the gala, at least not directly."

"What...what is it then?"

"I have something to give you," he said as he pulled a small jewelry box from his pocket. And there's an incredible story that goes along with this."

Prudy looked at him quizzically.

He opened the jewelry box and presented it to Prudy, who took the box and stared at the gorgeous gold pearl and citrine ring it held inside.

"It's absolutely gorgeous! Where did you get this?"

"Gertrude had to do some minor alterations on the tuxedo. When she was cleaning up the jacket, she felt something in the pocket. She pulled this out and was stunned when she realized it had to be the ring that matched the citrine necklace. The fact that it was in the mayor's pocket of the tuxedo he wore for special occasions, she assumed he'd had every intention of giving it to his wife but was not able to do so because he died before he had the chance."

"Oh, my goodness. But how can we be sure the ring was for Alexandra, and not perhaps someone else?"

"By someone else do you mean Amelia?"

"Yes, that awful thought did cross my mind."

"No, no way,"

"You sound awfully sure about that."

"With good reason. I promise you. Prudy, there are two very good reasons why I'm certain the ring was purchased by Samuel for his beloved Alexandra."

"Please tell me what they are."

"First, the ring has a citrine in it which is a match to the one in the necklace, like they are meant to be a set."

"Yes, okay...and the other reason?"

Dylan gently took the box from Prudy and removed the ring from it. He read the inscription on the inside of the band of the ring. "This one is not in French. It says, *For Alexandra, All my love always ~S.*"

Prudy smiled, because at that precise moment in time she knew without a doubt that Alexandra and Samuel had been very much in love. Alexandra appearing to them during the séance and what was written in Amelia's journal proved Alexandra did not murder her husband. Prudy held back a tear as emotions flooded through her, feeling a sense of grief over her great aunt and uncle's unfortunate murders. How happy they would have been to have grown old together had they been given the opportunity.

"Prudy, I investigated a bit more and found out that the mayor's and Alexandra's wedding anniversary was June 16th. Samuel died on June 15th, 1897. He'd probably been planning to take his wife out to celebrate their anniversary and give her this ring. So, he put it in the pocket of this tuxedo, the suit he wore for special occasions, and planned on giving it to Alexandra over dinner. But he never got the chance to give it to her. Look at the ring. Although it's very old, it looks brand new. That's because it's been in this pocket for over a hundred years and it's never been worn."

Prudy smiled as she took the ring from Dylan and looked at the inscription. "It is gorgeous."

"I want you to have the ring, Prudy."

Prudy stared at Dylan in disbelief. "But I'm sure it cost a fortune," Prudy said as she again touched the citrine necklace she was wearing. "And you already gave me this beautiful necklace."

"I called Gertrude to thank her for everything, and we discussed the story behind the ring. She wants you to have it. Besides, she joked and told me since she found it in the tuxedo pocket, that I was meant to have it. And since Samuel was unable to give it to Alexandra, that I should give it to you. So, can I put it on your finger? I'm sure that's what Samuel would have done. He would have presented the ring to Alexandra and then placed it on her finger."

"Oh Dylan, it's so beautiful. But I'm not sure it will fit me."

"I have a positive feeling the ring will fit you just fine." Dylan said as he slipped it on the ring finger of Prudy's right hand.

"It's a perfect fit, and the necklace and the ring worn together are a beautiful set."

"It doesn't surprise me at all that the ring fits you, Prudy.

"I don't know what to say, Dylan. Except, thank you. This ring and the necklace mean so much to me. I will treasure them always."

Dylan smiled serenely and then put his arms around Prudy. He drew her to him, and they kissed. When the kiss ended, Dylan said, "You know, I think Samuel and Alexandra are looking down on us right now, and I truly believe they are together and happy. I also think everything that's happened has turned out exactly as it was supposed to."

"You mean like we're fulfilling destiny?"

"Something like that, yes. Now, Miss Trivit, I believe you promised that we would have one glass of wine before we left for the gala. I must confess that I do have a slight case of the jitters."

"Oh yes, I think that would be a good idea. I could use a glass to calm my nerves as well." Prudy looked at the clock. But we'll have to drink up. We should arrive at the gala a few minutes before seven."

Dylan followed Prudy out to the kitchen. The bottle of Merlot was in the cupboard. She poured them each a short glass of the deep burgundy wine.

"Here you go. This should do the trick."

"Thank you, miss. I propose a toast. To Samuel and Alexandra Beaudicort," Dylan said as he lightly touched his glass to the one Prudy was holding, which slipped a bit in her grasp, and some of the dark, burgundy wine splashed out of the glass and onto the bodice of her gown.

"Oh no!"

Dylan took the glass Prudy was holding. "Prudy, I'm so sorry! Let me help you clean that up right away."

"It's not your fault, Dylan. The glass just seemed to slip right out of my hand. I'll get a towel wet with some cold water and try to blot it up from the fabric."

"What can I do to help?"

"Well, the gown will be wet from the water. Could you run upstairs and get my hairdryer out of the bathroom?"

"Sure thing."

Prudy held a kitchen towel under the faucet and then dabbed at the stained fabric. Thankfully, it was coming out, but she was getting the gown quite wet. By the time Dylan came back downstairs with the hairdryer, the deep, red stain was gone, but replacing the wine stain was now a big, wet spot.

Dylan plugged in the hairdryer and handed it to Prudy, who turned it on and blew the hot air on the wet area of the gown. Dylan waited patiently.

"It's amazing the stain came out."

"Yes, it is. But this fabric is dense and it's taking quite a while to dry."

Prudy looked at the clock in the kitchen, and to her dismay, it was 6:45 p.m. "We should have left ten minutes ago. We just can't be late!"

Dylan looked closely at her gown. "It looks almost dry. Let's go! We can open the car windows, and it should be completely dry by the time we get there."

Prudy turned off and unplugged the hairdryer. They hurried back into the living room where she grabbed her evening bag, and they ran out of the door and quickly got in the car. It was 6:50 p.m.

Chapter Twenty-Seven

Maggie paced back and forth outside of the main door to the Mystic Port Museum, impatiently waiting for her niece and Dylan to arrive. They were definitely late. Where could they be? She looked at her watch for the third time. It was 6:55 p.m. She was getting seriously worried. She knew something had to be wrong. There was no way Prudy would be late. Not for this.

Gertrude rushed out the door. "Maggie, any sign of them?"

"No, and I can't understand it. If there was something wrong, Prudy would have called me. She wouldn't want me to worry."

"Perhaps in all the excitement she forgot her cell phone. Maybe they're on their way. I told Gilbert to keep an eye out in case they enter through the back. When they get here and take their places in the center of the ballroom, he will start the band. They're warming up right now."

Maggie looked anxiously at Gertrude. "Yes, I can hear them. Gosh, I hope they weren't in an accident or there was some other mishap."

Gertrude put her hand on her friend's shoulder. "I'm sure they'll be along any minute."

Maggie started pacing but then stopped short. She shot Gertrude a shocked look when she heard the band start to play the waltz that Prudy and Dylan were supposed to dance to.

Gertrude said, in a relieved tone, "They must have been running late and gone directly into the ballroom through the back. Gilbert would not have started the band playing unless Prudy and Dylan had arrived. Thank goodness!"

Both ladies hurried to the crowded ballroom. The crowd standing around the outside perimeter made it difficult for them to see Prudy and Dylan on the dance floor. The two ladies weaved in and around the crowd until they finally found a spot where they could more clearly see the extraordinary couple as they appeared to glide around the dance floor.

"My God, if I didn't know any better I'd swear that was Alexandra and the mayor. Prudy and Dylan must have really practiced this waltz," Maggie said excitedly.

Gertrude smiled at her friend. "Maybe that's why they were running late. They were practicing the dance."

When the dancing couple glided over to the side of the ballroom where the ladies were standing, both of them got a much better look at the amazing couple. At the same moment, they both gasped as they realized that something very strange was happening. Who were these imposters?

Maggie thought her knees were going to buckle. She held onto Gertrude as if her life depended on it. Gertrude held her up.

"I can't believe what I'm seeing. Good lord, who is that?"

Gertrude squinted, then gasped in disbelief. "I'd like to know what's going on here."

"So would I," said Dylan in a hushed tone."

In their concentrated focus on the dancing couple, neither Gertrude nor Maggie had seen Prudy and Dylan as they walked up and stood behind them.

Prudy held tightly onto Dylan. "This is unbelievable. Are you thinking what I'm thinking?"

"Are you thinking this is a ghostly visitation of the best kind by your great aunt and the mayor?"

"I...I believe so, yes."

Some of the people in the crowd overheard Prudy and Dylan talking. People started whispering in disbelief. Others thought it was a stunt. Some, who hadn't seen them enter the room, didn't notice anything strange at all. As the song came to an end, the dancing couple glided slowly towards the expanse of French doors at the far end of the ballroom. Hand in hand they seemed to float through the glass doors and then dissipated into thin air. There was an almost unison gasp from many in the crowd of onlookers.

Prudy smiled and a tear ran down her cheek. Dylan shook his head in disbelief. Maggie, who had almost fainted, was fanning herself slowly with the antique fan she'd borrowed from Gertrude, who was clinging onto her friend in a state of bewildered shock.

Prudy quietly said to Dylan, her aunt, and Gertrude, "I believe Alexandra and Samuel are now together, knowing their legacy will live on. I'm hoping there will now be peace and no more hauntings, either at the house or the museum. Although, I wouldn't mind if Aunt Alexandra paid me a visit every once in awhile."

A few people turned to Prudy and demanded to know if that had been part of the show. A man standing behind her started to clap. "That was the best hologram I've ever seen. It looked absolutely real. Well done, Miss Trivit!"

Dylan added, "Yes, a truly unforgettable moment to be sure." He kissed Prudy on the cheek and then said quietly, "And to think I was nervous about having to dance in front of all these people."

Prudy smiled at Dylan, and they all laughed. She led Dylan out to the center of the dance floor as Gilbert announced, "Miss Trivit invites you to join in the festivities as we all celebrate together this very monumental occasion for our town."

The End

BWL Author
Betty Ann Harris

A self-admitted romantic, Betty Ann Harris also enjoys a good suspense story. Combining the two, her most favorite genre is romantic suspense. But she also delves into the world of paranormal romance and mysteries, because who doesn't love a good ghost story or murder mystery?

Standing on the edge of danger, running away from the one she fears, and falling for the one who is trying to save her. This is the basic idea of her romantic suspense books. If you crave romance but love suspense, then you'll enjoy her books.

It is her desire to keep readers involved in the story, to make them feel they are right there in the scene. She writes descriptively about and uses dramatic settings. She also loves keeping her reader's attention by building suspense and throwing twists and turns in the plot. Hopefully, you'll be on the edge of your seat!

Go ahead, get swept away!

Website:
http://ladylizzie1.wix.com/authorbettyannharris

Facebook:
https://www.facebook.com/AuthorBettyAnnHarris

BWL Publishing

bwlpublishing.ca